FILE M FOR MURDER

FILE M FOR MURDER

A CORNELIA UPSHAW AND FANCY MYSTERY

INDIA EDGHILL

Five Star • Waterville, Maine

First Edition
First Printing: December 2004

Published in 2004 in conjunction with
Tekno Books and Ed Gorman.

Set in 11 pt. Plantin by Minnie B. Raven.

Printed in the United States on permanent paper.

Library of Congress Cataloging-in-Publication Data

Edghill, India.
    File M for murder : a Cornelia Upshaw and Fancy
mystery / by India Edghill.—1st ed.
        p. cm.
    ISBN 1-59414-190-8 (hc : alk. paper)
    1. Women detectives—New York (State)—New York—
Fiction.   2. Executives—Crimes against—Fiction.
3. Temporary employees—Fiction.   4. New York (N.Y.)—
Fiction.   5. Single mothers—Fiction.   6. Secretaries—
Fiction.   I. Title.
PS3555.D474F55 2004
819′.54—dc22   2004042395

For all those Type-A executives for whom I worked as a temporary secretary and who unwittingly provided the inspiration for this series;

For Bast, who would never dream of shopping at Mirror, Mirror;

For Nicole Jordan, who ensured Cornelia didn't drink Diet Pepsi;

Above all, for Rosemary Edghill, without whom this book would have no plot.

And also, now, for my beloved Harry (Britt Tax Deduction at Mooncoign) and Bella (Britt Silver Bell at Mooncoign), who have taught me the joys of living life with a true Cavalier Attitude.

PROLOGUE

Perhaps I should begin this story with those magic words "once upon a time," for telling it now, it seems that I lived in a fairy-tale world—a golden age roughly two decades in our past, an age that lacked such modern amenities as cell phones, e-mail, and color-coded terrorism alert levels. As you will see, for many reasons, this story could not have happened now. But in those halcyon days when it was still the twentieth century—days that now seem so long ago and far away—these things could happen, and did.

As the opening line of *The Go-Between* so aptly puts it, "The past is a foreign country."

We did things differently there.

CHAPTER ONE

FRIDAY EVENING

I learned the hard way that there's really only one choice you get to make in this life: whether to sell Them your body or your soul.

Having made the other mistake once, I now choose to sell Them my body. In other words, I'm a secretary. Nowadays They get my body from nine to five—longer, if they're willing to pay through the nose for it to Metropolitan Office Professionals. I'm a professional temporary secretary, and I'm very, very good.

I can type swiftly and accurately, and take dictation too, and I know what "alphabetical order" means. I can also operate almost any word processing system currently in use, and a number of those that are now considered passé, except by the poor fool of an office manager who got suckered into buying the Cutting Edge that dulled so quickly. I can also answer a telephone promptly and politely.

Don't laugh—today the number of people who both can and are willing to do these things is shrinking rapidly. Everyone wants to love his/her work. I love my paycheck.

As I said, I do secretarial work from nine to five, Monday through Friday, and I get well paid for my efficiency. MOP knows a good thing when it tests it. And then at five I walk out the door of whatever office I'm currently working at free and clear.

This attitude drives a lot of people right round the twist

(as the British branch of my family says), especially neo-feminist managerial women. They just can't believe that someone with my (and here I modestly quote) intelligence, education, and organizational abilities really wants to work as a secretary. I could really *make* something of myself. (My mother agrees, except that *she* thinks I should make something of myself by marrying again—which I will do about the time there's ice dancing in Hell.) It's my opinion that I already have made something of myself. Something that *I* like.

Anyway, that particular very hot New York City summer my assignment was a six-week stint at Dayborne Ventures, Inc. Dayborne Ventures was an extremely prestigious, high-ticket company that did something truly magnificent in the way of international finance. I wasn't quite sure what. In my more cynical moments, I sometimes suspected even the regular Dayborne employees weren't quite sure what. But whatever Dayborne's business was, running it kept its employees on their collective toes. At Dayborne, a harassed manager was a happy manager.

As you might guess from the above, Dayborne was extremely—not to say passionately—corporate, and proud of it. The firm occupied three entire floors of a soaring glass-and-steel tower in the financial district a block from Wall Street. Through the floor-to-ceiling walls of glass to the north, you could see most of Manhattan; to the south, there was a magnificent view of the harbor. East and west looked only over Brooklyn and New Jersey, respectively; unimportant territory.

Within the glass tower, Dayborne's corporate taste ran to cutting edge decor and wave-of-the-future technology. Reception was an engineer's dream of polished steel walls and charcoal gray carpet, and the receptionist's desk looked like a starship console. Past the heavy glass doors into Dayborne proper, shades of cool blue-gray reigned supreme. Walls, carpets, secretarial furniture all coordinated.

Doors to executive offices were polished teak, and the executive offices themselves were supplied with the most intimidating power-trip furniture money could buy. Upon the walls hung, at precisely calculated intervals, works of art that just happened to coordinate with the office color scheme.

Everything was so elegantly low-key and tasteful it occasionally made me want to spray-paint the walls in Day-Glo neon stripes.

This wasn't to say Dayborne Ventures was a bad place to work, just that I found a little of Dayborne went a very long way. Fortunately, I was only there for most of June and almost all of July, while someone named Annabel Price, who was something called the Assistant Secretary to Ms. Fran Jenkins, Executive Secretary to Mr. J. Abercrombie Davis, Executive Vice President, had her baby. I do have to admit that Dayborne had not only magnificent views, but equally magnificent air-conditioning. New York City sweltered under the hottest June since—well, since the last one—and I was truly grateful for Dayborne's corporate cool, if for nothing else.

And for six weeks you can put up with practically anything.

Including the obligatory, "No, really, Cornelia—you have such *potential*" speech.

(My temporary bosses and co-workers *will* call me Cornelia, although when I'm working I prefer to be called Mrs. Upshaw. I think it adds a nice touch of efficient distance to business relationships that are, by their very nature, temporary. Sometimes I get my way on this, sometimes I don't. Although why the Corporate Powers That Be insist that We're All Jolly Friends Together with one breath and then with the next complain that This Is A Business, You Know, I've never figured out. One or the other. You can't have both at once.)

I'd heard the Obligatory You Have Such Potential Speech at least half-a-dozen times during the three weeks I'd so far been at Dayborne. The young, upwardly-mobile female executives were all eager to mentor—the new trend in managerial meddling. Now everyone who hopes to be a real player someday yearns to be a Mentor, a Role Model, and (don't laugh) to acquire his or her very own Mentee. Yes, that is indeed how they phrase it. Apparently the word "protégé" is obsolete, and possibly actionable. The first time I heard someone say, "Jane is my mentee," I'm afraid I did not manage to keep an entirely businesslike expression on my face, a gaffe I camouflaged by developing the worst coughing fit of my entire career to date. I'd explained the coughing by saying, "Allergies," and did not expand upon this by adding that I was allergic to bastard neologisms.

This afternoon, the Obligatory YHSP Speech was being made by Harriet Benson, who was the current advocate of upgrading Upshaw. The other Dayborne women who'd cornered me and urged me on to glory and ulcers had abandoned the effort fairly easily when I declined, with thanks, to be Upgraded. They had done their duty to Female Empowerment and Sisterhood, and if I didn't want to be Empowered, they'd find some underachieving woman who did.

But Harriet Benson was different. Alas, Harriet really, truly *cared*.

Harriet was about my age, or maybe a little younger: twenty-eight and already an assistant vice president. At Dayborne Ventures they gave out AVP's the way a pediatrician gives out lollipops, and for the same reason: good be-havior. Harriet Benson took everything corporate- and career-related very, very seriously. And the second she'd set eyes on me, she'd decided to be very, very serious about my future. I understood her point of view: like Rhett Butler, Harriet Benson hated to see waste, and she regarded my casual attitude towards the business world as sheer waste. If I'd believed Harriet's exhortations, I'd have to consider my refusal to lift my sights from secretarial to managerial as a tragedy worthy of Euripides' pen.

Apparently AVP Benson had five free minutes this Friday afternoon, and planned to use those precious moments to attempt once more to raise my consciousness and show me the glories of the fast track to success. "You know, you could do a lot better for yourself, Cornelia—"

"Mrs. Upshaw," I murmured without either rancor or much hope of affecting Harriet's form of address. Especially since Harriet was magnanimously overlooking the fact that I was a Mere Secretary, and condescending to address me as an equal. Sort of.

"You've got the talent, the brains—you know we have a management trainee program, don't you? Why don't you apply?"

Well, for one thing, because I like to work only thirty-five hours a week. (I'd rather be independently wealthy, but I'll settle for being independent.) And because I already *have* a full-time life which suits me very well. But I didn't say this, because as far as I could see, Harriet Benson, AVP, could say the same thing about her own lifestyle choice. Different strokes, as they say.

"You'd be just perfect," Harriet continued. "I'd be glad to recommend you, if you'd like."

"Thank you," I said politely. I was raised to be polite; a

Perfect Little Southern Lady. Besides, Harriet was trying to be nice, and I knew it never even occurred to her that she shouldn't be dangling Dayborne careers in front of a temp without authorization from both her superiors here and mine at MOP. So to change the subject, I asked Harriet what she was doing over the weekend.

"Oh, I'll be here—Davis wants the spreadsheets on AIB&C first thing Monday."

I would have commiserated with Harriet if I'd thought she was in the least sorry to be losing an entire irreplaceable weekend to AIB&C (which I had learned stood for the vitally-important Accounts International Billing and Charges subdepartment) and a computer. But in a way, I understood Harriet—understood her all too well. Harriet regarded Dayborne the way I'd once regarded my late husband Ravenal. I just hoped Harriet wouldn't someday be as disappointed in her perfect corporation as I'd been in my perfect hero. Love's Young Dream has a nasty habit of mutating into Maturity's Nightmare.

So I smiled at Harriet and told her to have fun, and then carefully placed the cover over the electronic typewriter, unplugged the computer keyboard and stowed it in its special drawer in the desk, and made sure my desktop was empty and the drawers were locked. Dayborne Ventures was what they called "security-conscious" and I called "paranoid." Nobody, as far as I could tell, had the least idea what Dayborne Ventures *did*, so I didn't see how any of it could be of any use to anybody outside the firm. It was little enough use to those inside it.

On the other hand, Dayborne's attitude meant that even such an ephemeral employee as I was got a key to the desk that was temporarily hers. This was a feature I liked. To recoin a phrase: always lock your desk; take your keys.

Then I beat it out of there. Because Harriet's Mr. Davis, head of the department I was currently working for, had a cute little trick I'd discovered the first week of my stint at Dayborne. Just before quitting time on almost any Friday, J. Abercrombie Davis would come sauntering along with a major project that just *had* to be done before his secretarial staff left. Said projects usually involved overseas transport of papers to a part of the world in which everybody was already in bed, or had just started week-long holidays that mandated closing down all electrical connections to the outside world. In either case, it always seemed to me that the Vital Information could just as well be sent the next business day, instead of running into overtime.

But Mr. Davis didn't see it that way—which was, no doubt, why he was an Executive Vice President working on hypertension and an ulcer and I was only a Temporary Secretary working (at the moment) on reading my way through the collected works of Anthony Trollope.

But apparently this Friday Davis hadn't managed to get any vital material in under the wire; Fran Jenkins, his Executive Secretary, was also closing up. I looked back as I opened the heavy glass door to Reception and saw her shutting drawers and turning keys with firm, deliberate movements. And it only 5:00, too.

Which was rather amazing, as I'd begun to think Fran was shackled to her desk. I'm a secretary of the Old School (as I said, I can type using all ten fingers), but Frances Jenkins was a secretary of the *very* Old School: totally efficient, totally discreet, and totally devoted to her boss's interests. She came by these attributes naturally, as Fran was somewhere over fifty, plenty old enough to be most of the Dayborne secretarial staff's mother. Her wardrobe didn't do anything to dispel this illusion; Fran wore matronly and

15

oddly outdated polyester suits in falsely girlish colors like baby's breath pink and faded mint green. Under the stiff jackets she wore ruffled blouses that she accessorized with a string of pearls. I suspected the pearls were imitation.

Now I waited for her, holding the door invitingly. "Come on. I don't see him anywhere."

Fran came puffing up—she was plump and soft, and any exertion whatsoever caused her shortness of breath. I could not imagine why a nice lady like Fran was at Dayborne, which apparently tested its secretaries by passing them through the eye of a needle, unless it was because Fran was the only secretary they'd ever found who could work with J. Abercrombie Davis without going mad. Fran hesitated, and I added encouragingly, "I think he must have left early."

He had, after a manner of speaking, but we didn't find that out until Monday.

"Well . . ." Fran began doubtfully, and then seemed to gain courage. "If we don't see him, I suppose we can leave."

I supposed we could, since it was, after all, quitting time. Nor did I wonder where Davis might lurk; this time he'd missed his chance to spring upon us at the last possible moment before the elevator doors slid closed. And I had much, much better things to think about this evening than the whereabouts of a temporary boss. It was Friday, it was summertime, it was 5:00.

I was free.

My first stop on the way home was at Metropolitan Office Professionals. MOP is located in the top two floors—and the roof—of an ex-factory in an unfashionable Manhattan neighborhood halfway between Midtown and the Lower East Side—the sort of neighborhood composed of co-ops lived in by yuppies who are never home and by re-tail stores whose ownership changes as regularly as the seasons.

The building has an elevator, but it frequently isn't working, and I like to take the stairs for the exercise anyway. So I climbed up six flights and breezed into MOP's lobby—a large open area that still manages to look like a redecorated factory loft, no matter how many spider plants and mauve movable walls MOP hopefully puts in. Maybe it's the tangle of pipes writhing across the ceiling like demented metal garter snakes.

On the other hand, there's certainly plenty of space, a good deal of which I had to cross in order to get to the receptionist's desk. In addition to the cheerful receptionist, Krissie, sitting ready with a stack of neatly labeled white envelopes containing the weekly paychecks, Holly Steinberg was there, stuffing papers into her already overladen briefcase.

"Oh, hi, Cornelia. How's the Dayborne job going?"

"Great," I said, "except for the boss."

"What's wrong with him?" Holly regarded me anxiously, her brown eyes wide and her brown hair seeming extra-curly with concern. Holly's my "placement counselor" at MOP, and is very protective of "her people." She's an awfully nice girl, and I always get a kick out of watching her try to mother and protect me—I'm several years older and at least six inches taller than she is.

"Nothing," I assured her, "except that he's a complete son-of-a-witch."

Even after all this time in New York, that's the last vestige of Southern speech pattern that I just can't shake. Other expletives can and do roll trippingly from my tongue, but I still can't bring myself to call someone a "bitch." Not that we Southerners are mealy-mouthed, mind—the first time a New Yorker heard me cuss someone out and end an extremely frank description of the creep's relationship to his mother with the words "son-of-a-witch," he nearly choked to death on his white wine spritzer. And my sister Lizard's pejorative vocabulary can be quite Elizabethan in its earthiness.

"That's all?" Holly asked. "No touchy-feely stuff?"

I assured her that Mr. J. Abercrombie Davis never made inappropriate sexual advances or innuendos—at least, not to me.

"Oh, no, nothing like that—he just always has this last-minute project that he managed to forget about all week, or needs his secretary to come in at seven a.m. and then he doesn't get there till nine—that sort of thing."

Which Mr. Personality even pulled on me, even though I'm a temp and the overtime would hit him where it really hurt—in the budget.

In case you don't know how a temporary office help agency works, I'll explain. The average temp agency charges the firm hiring a secretary from them precisely twice what the temp agency pays that secretary. MOP's billing practices are slightly different: they pay their temp personnel less than the going hourly rate and charge the hiring firms triple that rate, not double.

For example, since I'm paid ten dollars an hour (as I mentioned before, my skills make me a high-ticket item), this means Dayborne pays MOP thirty dollars for each hour I work. This is certainly more than Dayborne pays its own secretaries.

It's true that ten dollars an hour—$350 a week before taxes—doesn't sound like much. In fact, it isn't much, considering that I could walk myself over to almost any of the major firms and make more than twice that as an executive secretary to some hyperactive Type-A boss. I could, in fact, make more by working for the average temp agency, instead of for MOP.

But there are three reasons I work for Metropolitan Office Professionals instead. One is the health insurance. The second reason I work for MOP is that I can (with care) afford to. And there's a third reason, the most important one.

You see, MOP's administrative offices occupy the sixth floor of that old factory building in that less-than-fashionable neighborhood. Their free childcare facility occupies the seventh floor. The playground is on the roof, which is also MOP territory.

The third reason I work for MOP is three years old, and her name is Heather Melissa Upshaw.

Heather is also the reason I live in New York now, rather than in Charleston. Call me a coward, but after my husband died, I just couldn't face the family pressure to create a perfect widowhood to complement my perfect marriage.

My perfect mistake: my marriage to my second cousin, Ravenal Kennard Upshaw. Raving Rav, who'd been the handsomest thing in three counties. He'd been tall and dark and hot-eyed and sort of dangerous looking, like a sullen angel or a temperamental panther. All the girls were mad for him, of course.

And to this day, I still don't know why, really, Ravenal thought he wanted to marry *me*. For one thing, I didn't look in the least like a proper Southern Belle. In my heart of hearts, I liked to pretend I was elegant, like Lauren Bacall—who is not exactly the *belle ideal* of the Old South.

In fact, I was (and still am) tallish and thinnish and need quite a lot of makeup to disguise the fact that my eyelashes are practically invisible. And I got better marks in school

19

than Ravenal did, which wasn't difficult. I don't think he
ever cracked open a book.

No, he'd gotten by on charm. In Ravenal's defense, I
will say that I fancied myself heart-over-heels in love with
him. But I'd always acted very cool around him; I knew
Cousin Ravenal only had eyes for kittenish girls with large
bosoms and small minds. Maybe he thought I was a chal-
lenge.

Anyway, we got married when I was eighteen (right out
of high school) and he was twenty-two (right out of college.
He'd even managed to graduate. I wonder who wrote his
papers for him?). We had the biggest, splashiest, most *ante-
bellum chic* wedding of the year: a dozen bridesmaids and a
ring-bearer in velvet knee-breeches and a darling little
flower girl in a dress that made her look like a miniature
Scarlett O'Hara. I wore white, of course—I was even entitled to the non-color. My dress had a hoop skirt big enough
to camp out in. I wore great-grandmother Contessa's
Alençon lace wedding veil.

To cut a long and pretty common story short, our marriage didn't last. To put it at its kindest, Ravenal and I
wanted different things out of life. I wanted a husband, a
home, children. I also wanted to go to college.

Raving Rav wanted to go on Living The Legend.

His script was clichéd, but it suited Rav just fine, because as I later realized, Ravenal too was a cliché. He liked
fast cars, fast women, fast spending.

Peter Pan on amphetamines.

And as for the physical side of married life—well, the
erotic delights my perfervid girlish imagination had dwelt
upon lovingly before our marriage were part of the Ravenal
legend, but like most legends, they didn't really exist.
Ravenal was really only interested in himself, and my

clumsy devotion bored him. (All right, I'll admit it; eventually he called me frigid. At the time, it hurt like hell.)

But I did my immature and naive best to be a Good Wife To Ravenal. Not an easy task, but I persevered. Later I realized I'd been a damn fool, and hadn't done Ravenal any particular good either, but I did derive a certain useful experience out of the whole deal.

I kept house and covered for him to his boss and his relatives. After a while, when I realized that there was *never* going to be the time or money for me to attend local college classes ("Hey, you're my *wife*. My wife doesn't have to go to school like some little kid. Besides, you've got the whole damn house filled with your goddamn books anyway. Go read some of them."), I started sneaking money out of the housekeeping funds so I could attend what I could: part-time courses at the local business school.

Looking back on those eternally vivid years, I can see a woman subconsciously preparing to bolt; one sensible enough to know she'd need some saleable job skills. At the time, I just wanted to be doing *something* besides reading all day and worrying over what Ravenal was up to now. And I salved my conscience by using what I'd learned to help Ravenal, because he couldn't keep a secretary for long and work he brought home with him just sat until he got around to it, which could take him quite a while.

So I started doing secretarial work for him. I also rewrote his reports, which I don't think he even noticed. Oddly enough, he never asked where, when, or how I'd picked up these useful skills. Those around Ravenal Lived To Serve, an attitude he never in all his fleeting life learned to question.

As I said, Ravenal got by on charm—and on people like me, who'd do anything for him. He would have made the world's most successful con man if he'd only had any actual ambition, but he remained an amateur to the end. I was too young to see that I wasn't helping Ravenal's character any with my doormat act.

Which role, of course, I grew pretty sick of playing as I grew up and he didn't. I know this is the ultimate modern marriage cliché; in our case, it was true. Ravenal didn't age well. Or gracefully. Or, in the end, at all.

The final break came when I discovered I was pregnant.

Heather was an accident, of course. Ravenal had never wanted to be tied down by kids. And by that time Ravenal and I rarely engaged in any marital relations other than fighting. But he'd come home drunk and sorry for himself because his boss had been mean to him and because his latest lady friend had just told him good-bye, and I'd been sitting home and to be perfectly honest I'd had a bourbon or two myself. And that's how our daughter was conceived.

I waited until I was really sure before I told Ravenal. I was delighted; I was still just idiotically optimistic enough to think that a child would miraculously repair our shattered marriage.

Ravenal told me to go get an abortion. I told him to go to hell. I said a lot of other things, too: all true. Ravenal hauled off and knocked me down. It was the first time he hit me, and the last. He tried to kick me, too.

Sheer rage brought me up like a cat; I grabbed the first thing that came to hand and belted the side of his handsome head with it. I'd clobbered him with a big heavy book that stopped him in his tracks; academic presses use quality paper.

"Touch us again, and I'll kill you." I still remember the sound of my own voice, and it's not something I ever want to hear again: a low raspy growl, flat and deadly. "Get out of this house. Now."

I took a step forward; I must have looked like Medea, or one of the Furies. Ravenal got.

I heard the door slam and the roar of his Jaguar XK6 as he floored the temperamental car and whipped it out of the drive. I was too conscientious to drink while I was pregnant, so I went and lay down on my bed and stared at the ceiling and didn't think about anything until the State Trooper came to the door later that night to tell me that my husband Ravenal had wrapped his Jaguar around a tree.

After the funeral, I moved north, joining my sister in the Big Apple. My hard-earned office skills and old-fashioned education (translation: I actually could read, write a clear English sentence, and add a column of figures without a calculator) could have won me a place in almost any firm in the city. But I couldn't face the bonds of another permanent relationship, even with an employer. I turned to temp work instead. Metropolitan Office Professionals was more than happy to make my acquaintance, and I was purely delighted to join the ranks of the few, the proud, the MOPs.

Because, along with health insurance, Metropolitan Office Professionals offered free day care. Free day care is even more unusual in the temp business than health insurance. In fact, MOP is the only agency I've ever heard of that offers this enticing and well-nigh irresistible benefit.

When I arrived in the Big Apple as a new widow, I was (in the old-fashioned parlance my family revels in using) "in the family way." Knowing I'd need an employer willing to be flexible about hours and time off, I assessed my skills, studied my options, and then interviewed at every temporary employment agency listed in the Manhattan Yellow Pages. By the time I reached the "M's," I was getting pretty discouraged. And then I called Metropolitan Office Professionals.

Holly Steinberg at MOP was the first "placement counselor" I'd talked to who didn't promptly lose all interest in me when I told her I was expecting a child. Instead, she perked up even more—Holly has more energy than I think the law actually allows—and began telling me all about MOP's wonderful benefits package. "We like to think of MOP as a family," Holly said, and I was so relieved at hearing that MOP had on-site babysitting that I didn't even think, "Look, honey, I already *have* a family and I'm up here to escape them." In fact, I smiled blissfully and said, "Where do I sign up?"

And I've been with MOP ever since—and even during the months I was on hiatus after Heather Melissa was born, MOP kept me on their payroll list. During the first year of Heather's life, I mostly worked for MOP by doing typing at home. But by the time my darling daughter was walking, I knew it was time to get back to work outside the apartment, at least part-time. I love my sister dearly, but listening to Lizard when she's painting gets sort of wearing (artists, like most delicate, creative folk, have vocabularies that could strip wallpaper). And when the workroom has me typing at my word processor, Heather in her playpen, Lizard at her easel, and a cover model or two on the plywood dais, it's just a tad crowded. Mind, I didn't object to having the Stone Hunk of the Month lounging around as scenery while I typed. Flowing locks and bare buff torsos sure livened up time spent on dryly-verbose legal documents.

And watching Stone Hunk and Lady Fair assume backbreaking "romantic" poses and hold them without quiver or complaint as Lizard took photos or sketched taught me something about patience, too.

Anyway, its day care center is the reason MOP is located way downtown from all the other temporary employment agencies, which tend to cluster in midtown. MOP needed the space an old factory building provides. The day care is also the reason MOP has a die-hard core of fine, efficient workers who stay with them rather than flitting from agency to agency or off to the world of permanent employment in search of a benefits package and a larger paycheck. Workers like me.

So I was here at MOP this fine Friday afternoon to pick up both my paycheck and my daughter.

"Well, that's pretty typical," said Holly of my analysis of Mr. Davis's managerial flaws. "Just as long as he doesn't think you're fair game just because you're a temp."

"Holly, honey," I said, taking the long envelope containing my check from the receptionist, "*nobody* thinks that." I waved my left hand, making the broad gold band flash in the fluorescent light. "I just tell them it's *Mrs.* Upshaw, and they behave like perfect little gentlemen. Now stop worrying, and go home. It's Friday, you know."

"Yeah, I know." Holly sounded grim, as was only natural for one whose days—and sometimes whose evenings and even weekends—were frequently made hideous by frantic phone calls from desperate clients in urgent need of somebody *tomorrow.* "Look, *how* much longer are you at Dayborne?"

"Four more weeks," I told her. "Until just after the Second Quarter Closeout, whatever that is."

"Four weeks," she said gloomily. "Oh, well, I guess maybe I can get Danielle for this call-in. Want to work at a design studio?"

"Sure," I said, "as long as MOP's paying me." I waved the pay-envelope gently back and forth like a lady's fan before shoving it into my purse. "Have a good weekend; I've got to go up and get Heather."

Leaving Holly to her paper packing, I went back to the corridor and climbed up one more flight to the MOP childcare center. Pre- and after-school; bonded and licensed and very, very reliable. Leave your precious child with them with complete peace of mind.

Sound wonderful? It is—but MOP's management isn't run by altruistic fools; they own the best stable of temps and have the lowest turnover of any agency in the five boroughs.

I went through the double glass doors to the childcare center and stopped at the desk just inside to inform the receptionist that I was here to pick up Heather Upshaw. Jennifer, the MOP employee manning the day care desk, recognized me and smiled, and waved me on. If she hadn't known me, I would have had to show Jennifer my MOP photo ID; when, as occasionally happens, Lizard gets Heather for me, Lizard has to show a MOP-issued authorization card with her photo on it, a card I've countersigned. No one just walks in and collects a child "for my wife/husband/neighbor" here, for MOP is extremely conscientious and takes its responsibility for the children in its charge very seriously.

The seventh floor is entirely devoted to childcare. Since the children range in age from infant to teenager, their time spent there varying from all day to an hour or so after school, there's a lot involved in keeping them all safely and happily occupied. The seventh floor is divided into study rooms, play rooms, and a nursery. There's a reasonably well-stocked library of picture books and children's books both current and classic, as well as an extensive arts and crafts studio. A large indoor playground runs along the back half of the floor. The children are encouraged to amuse themselves constructively, which is why there's no television room. Occasionally the center will pull out the movie screen and the projector and show a movie, usually a Disney film or something from PBS, but only as a rare treat.

But since there are books, magazines, comic books (yes, really), coloring books, crayons, Lincoln logs, Erector sets, Play-Doh, building blocks, crossword puzzles, picture puzzles, games like Candyland, Snakes and Ladders, and Monopoly, plus poster paints, finger paints, and reams and reams of construction paper and gallons of glue, most of the kids seem to manage to amuse themselves just fine.

And frankly, I think the kids have more fun mucking about in the garden (potted plants indoors on the seventh floor and a larger spread, with vegetables as well as flowers, on the roof) and tending the menagerie (goldfish, newts, turtles, gerbils, a couple of guinea pigs, and some parakeets) than they do staring at a television screen. Somehow they can still tell you how to get to *Sesame Street*, so I don't think they're being deprived of any essential childhood experience.

The building's roof is part of the MOP childcare center, reached via either stairs or an elevator that travels only between the seventh floor and the roof. The roof serves as an outdoor playground, complete with jungle gym, swings, sandboxes, whirlarounds, and seesaws, as well as the aforementioned junior farmer's garden. There's no swimming pool, but one can't have everything.

Add in the kitchen, in which proper meals and healthy snacks are prepared, and some basic home ec is taught; mix in visiting storytellers; blend well with the fully trained and bonded staff, and you see why MOP's loyal and distinguished workforce is the wonder of temp agencies the length and breadth of the city. Mind, the other agencies could have the same kind of loyal and distinguished people on their payrolls if they'd do the same things MOP does. But that would mean two things temp agencies hate: spending money, and treating temps like real employees rather than as disposable and endlessly replaceable work units.

As my dear departed grandfather Wilkes Upshaw used to say as he bounced me on his knee, "You've got to spend money to make money." Grandpa Wil ought to know; he owned the best and most profitable construction business in Charleston for forty years.

Once past day care reception, I went over to the waiting room, where Heather (obviously freshly washed and tidied) greeted me rapturously. "Mommy, there was a DOGGIE here today!"

I glanced over Heather's head to the grandmotherly-looking woman monitoring parental pickups. "We had a Show And Tell from the Police Department, and the officer brought a police dog. Such a smart animal!" She smiled. "The children loved it."

"I want a pleece dog!" Heather announced.

I stooped and hugged Heather. "Honey, we're not the police. We can't have a police dog."

"I want to be the pleece!" Heather said promptly, and I laughed and rumpled her shining dark curls.

"Maybe when you grow up, sugar-pie," I said, and accepted the Macy's shopping bag containing Heather's latest art project she was carrying home to show Aunt Lizard. Heather waved goodbye to Grandmotherly Type and then to Jennifer, and we went down the seven flights of stairs with me helping her slide carefully down the elegant, if ancient, brass banister.

To save time, I will admit right now that my daughter is the delight of my life. Unlike her mother, Heather is angelically lovely, and shows every sign of becoming what is known where I come from as a "heartbreaker" when she's a bit older. Huge dark eyes surrounded by sinfully long lashes, wavy dark hair, skin like heavy cream; in looks, Heather fortunately takes after her father. Unlike her late father, Heather is willing to be pleased by almost anything, a talent she must have inherited from some other ancestor.

Eventually we reached the lobby, where Heather once more set her feet on *terra firma*. Then we went out into the shimmering heat of a late June afternoon and walked uptown, towards home.

"Lizard? You home?"

"Yaaa."

The answer echoed down the thirty-foot hallway. It was either Lizard or our Siamese cat, Waldo.

"We're home," I called out, which was pretty obvious. Heather dashed past me, eager to tell Aunt Lizard all about her day (the MOP pre-school group had made squirrels out of brown paper and, as a bonus for good behavior, had also learned to sort their Crayolas by color). Smiling, I began lugging the D'Agostino's bag down the long hall towards the kitchen.

I was named Cornelia, after one grandmother; my unfortunate sister was named Lispenard, after the other. These names were the fallout of a fit of optimism on the part of our parents: perhaps Grandmothers Cornelia and Lispenard would Remember Us in their wills.

Unfortunately, they did.

Grandmother Cornelia Caroline Upshaw bestowed upon me a twelve-piece sterling silver Victorian tea service so heavy and rococo that you risk a hernia if you presume to lift the lid of the teapot. The tea service crouches like a sullen beast of prey on the coffee table in the living room, as there's simply no other place to put the thing, and gives the unwary a nasty start when they come upon it unexpectedly in dim light.

Between the Service and Waldo, the living room is an interesting territory to negotiate.

Waldo was Grandmother Lispenard Wharton Mingott's legacy to *her* namesake. Waldo is a seal-point Siamese cat quite as heavy and rococo as the Service; Grandmother Lis had named him something long and impressive in Thai. After we'd had him for a week, we changed his name to Waldo Lydecker. It seemed to suit him better. The principal difference between the feline Waldo and his filmatic namesake is that *our* Waldo would be exceedingly delighted to see his neighbor's children devoured by wolves. He would then devour the wolves.

Occasionally people—usually people who've seen *Bell, Book, and Candle* too often—ask Lizard whether Waldo is her familiar. Lizard always says he's not because he's too lazy, whatever that means. But she told me once that she wouldn't dare. I don't blame her.

Nobody calls my sister Lispenard; she's been Lizard since the day she was christened. For the usual reason: I, at the tender age of three, could not be expected to pronounce "Lispenard" with any degree of accuracy. And as anyone with a name in the least unusual will agree, "Lizard" is infinitely preferable to what's on Lizard's birth certificate: Lispenard Evangeline.

Actually, Lizard suits her. Unlike me, she's small and quick and vivid and glistens with color, especially after a buying binge in the makeup department at Bloomingdale's.

When I got far enough down the hall to spot Liz, she was glittering in purple and gold and was actually wearing a dress.

"You look like the Assyrian. What's the occasion?"

"Julian and I are going to the movies." Lizard continued examining the brown paper squirrel, slightly crushed and damp from handling, that Heather had proffered for inspection. "Hey, honey, this is real nice. You've got a real good talent for color work."

Which was a tactful way of saying the squirrel's tail was painted in green and orange stripes. I went into the kitchen, set the bag on the table, and glanced at the calendar. Today's square was filled with arcane symbols that I recognized as Lizard's excuse for handwriting.

"And just when are you going to cram in a movie tonight?" I called, beginning to unpack the strawberries.

"After Vespers and before Circle. It's the new Arnie Schwarzenegger."

"What's this one called, *The Defenstrator*?"

"Something like that." Lizard darted into the kitchen and kissed my cheek. She reeked, not unpleasantly, of patchouli. "I'll be late. See ya."

"Have a good time," I said. "Here's some fresh Eye of Newt in case you need it." I put a jar of black olives into the refrigerator. "And don't forget—widdershins is *counter*clockwise."

"Yaa," said Lizard, and dashed off again.

Lizard likes to think she's a witch, and currently belongs to something called the First Church of Wicca Scientist (I swear I am not making this up). Julian is an Episcopalian minister with Saint Benedict's on East 65th Street. Lizard and Julian met at an AIDS outreach clinic, literally over a patient (who turned out to be Jewish and didn't want to see either of them), when *his* cross became inextricably entangled with *her* pentacle. You know what a cross is, I'm sure, and why a minister wears one. Well, a pentacle is the equivalent religious jewelry for witches, a sort of metal line-drawing five-pointed star in a circle. The last time we visited home, Lizard's silver pentacle gave two of our aunts Palpitations, because they were sure it was a Star of David and were not in the least soothed by our mother pointing out that, "At least with Jews you always know who their *people* are."

Anyway, Lizard and Julian have been Significant Others ever since that fateful (and tangled) meeting. This isn't, actually, as odd as it seems, especially in New York. They both share an interest in comparative religion, membership in a number of social work associations, and a detestation for the IRS vis-à-vis its stand on non-profit, charitable, and religious organizations that amounts to a mania and leads them to support some surprisingly unlikely groups.

Julian is also Julian Lovell of the Boston Lovells. The Lodges may talk to the Cabots if they like, and the Cabots to God; the Lovells won't talk to any of them. Julian blotted the family escutcheon permanently due to his democratic willingness to consider God his equal. Julian is also rather devastating in the Ashley-Wilkes/Lord-Peter-Wimsey fashion, and eminently suitable as a love object for anyone involved, as Lizard swears she is, in a Nature religion. Summer sunshine hair, eyes the mottled iridescent blue of the wings of certain exotic butterflies, skin like very pale spring honey—well, you get the picture, and a very attractive one it is, too.

Oh, yes, Julian and Lizard have one other thing in common: the opinion that I'm too cynical, and could use a good deity in my life. I've given up listening to Lizard on that one, although she hasn't given up nagging. And I'm afraid I deeply shocked the fair Julian when he asked me who my clergyman was, because I said "Reverend Randollph," and after that Julian never mentioned the topic again. At least to me. Unlike Lizard, Julian knows how to take a gentle hint. Julian was even polite enough to borrow one of the Reverend Randollph mysteries, just to see what I was talking about. (Or possibly, as the author of the Reverend Randollph mysteries was himself a Methodist bishop, Julian regarded this as a professional courtesy to a fellow cleric.) Whether he ever read the book or not, I don't know, as I was too polite to ask him.

There was the fading clatter of high-heels on the hardwood floor and the slam of the apartment door. I followed on back down the hallway to the door, Heather chasing after me to slide on the polished wood. There, I made sure all the locks were turned, shot, and bolted, and then turned to walk back to the front of the apartment.

Or, as I should say, The Apartment.

Because there was one more legacy from Grandmother Lispenard, one for which we could almost forgive her saddling Liz with Waldo. The Apartment. Which she had left, in her thoroughly documented and totally legal will, to "my faithful and beloved companion of many years."

In other words, to her dyspeptic Siamese cat.

Waldo.

Fortunately, it was a life tenancy only, or the entire matter would have wound up as one of those Dickensian legal cases that crawl on past the heat death of the known universe. As it was, it meant that Lizard owned (or would own, after Waldo's demise) a long, dark, pre-war apartment in the East Fifties. Which meant both Lizard and I lived rent-free. Which meant we both could go our own merry ways without too much let or hindrance from reality.

Don't ever let anyone tell you that money can't buy happiness. Have you ever noticed that those attempting to foist this philosophy off on the general unwealthy public are usually twice as rich as Croesus and have every intention of staying that way, their allegedly miserable personal lives notwithstanding?

Squeaking with delight, Heather slid past me again; a clever girl, she'd taken off her shoes to reduce friction. Her Hello Kitty socks gave great slide, especially in our hallway, which is, as mentioned, thirty feet long.

The hallway walls are still covered with their original wallpaper, something dimly Victorian. Sometimes we argue over what, precisely, the blobs of faded colors are. Lizard says they're pre-Freudian Rorschach blots; I say (prosaic to the last) that they're probably cabbage roses. Heather's vote wavers between bloodstains and big fuzzy spiders. Sometimes I think Heather watches too much television.

On the right-hand side of the hallway are rooms: bedroom (Lizard's), bathroom, bedroom (mine and Heather's), in that order. Since the apartment is pre-war (pre-Spanish-American War, we think), the rooms are lofty and spacious—a good thing, since the closets are slightly smaller than my high-school locker.

Once past those rooms, there's the kitchen (also pre-war; in this case, pre-War Of Unprovoked Northern Aggression—that's the Civil War to you Yankees). Then the apartment opens up into a room the full width of the apartment that must once have been used for Gracious Dining. We have other uses for that space, so we eat in the kitchen, which is large and also came to us equipped with an old and sturdy dinette set. Now half of the former dining room is a home office for me and half of it is Lizard's art studio. An archway closed by a set of glass doors etched with peacocks in splendor leads from the office/studio into the living room.

The living room is the largest room in the apartment, and the only one that looks out over the street, instead of over the side alley. The full width of the front wall is windows, the old-fashioned kind composed of dozens of tiny square panes of glass. The glass itself is so old, light wavers through like light seen underwater.

There is also, tucked behind the kitchen, a six-by-ten-foot cubicle once called "the maid's room." These days (since no modern maid would condescend to dwell in such a primitive cell) Lizard uses it to store her art supplies and canvases in various stages of completion.

Lizard, you see, works as a free-lance cover artist. Next time you're browsing at Brentano's or Scribner's, check out the fantasy books. The painting on the cover may have been done by Liz Upshaw. Liz's painting wasn't, yet, a living—but without rent to pay, she got by.

Didn't I say money could buy happiness? Or at least freedom, which is almost as good and twice as negotiable.

"Mommy, Mommy, come look!" Heather, demanding I admire Aunt Liz's latest masterpiece.

Detouring prudently around Waldo, who was lying in a large, malevolent, beige-and-brown coil in the geometric center of the living room rug, I came; I looked; I admired.

"Gee, that's awful pretty, honey," I said. Right now Lizard was working on a series of covers for the fantasy line at Flatiron Press, and the living room was strewn with canvases on which fire-breathing damsels threatened lovesick dragons. Or possibly it was the other way around. Lizard's a good artist, but when a book publisher's art department wants a "definitive look" for a line, all the covers tend to look alike. (You should see the covers Lizard did for Chantilly Romance's *Next Chance at Love* series sometime; whether the male lead was a tenth-century Viking , an eighteenth-century highwayman, or a twentieth-century sheikh, on an NCL cover, Our Hero wore a six-inch-wide embossed leather belt and blue spandex knee pants.)

"That's *me*," Heather cooed, sounding like a delighted pigeon. She pointed at a tiny elf holding something (a sugar lump, possibly) out to a particularly scaly dragon.

Our Lizard makes shameless use of the materials at hand—in her case, her long-suffering sister and semi-insufferable niece. Rather to everyone's surprise, Heather adores posing for Aunt Lizard. In fact, Lizard calls Heather the best model she's ever had, which always strikes me as odd, since patience has never been one of the Upshaw virtues. I don't know where Heather gets hers from. Sometimes I worry about that girl.

I agreed that the glitter-clad elf looked suspiciously familiar, and leaned forward as if to inspect the image more closely.

"*Mustn't* touch," Heather warned me darkly. "Because it'll *smudge*."

"And Aunt Lizard'll turn you into a frog," I said, swooping my daughter up and nuzzling her cheek. Heather regarded me with the fond superiority of the pre-schooler who has not yet been taught to believe in utter nonsense.

"It's Friday. I want ice cream for dinner," she announced.

Friday nights, Heather chooses dinner. Usually it's ice cream, which is all right with me. Fortunately, I don't have to worry about what I eat, remaining what my Southern female relatives call "scrawny" no matter what I ingest in the way of empty-yet-delicious calories; we all get at least one

36

blessing to ameliorate our trials here on earth.

"Okay," I said. "Where shall we go for this ice cream?" As if I didn't know.

"*Ben-n-Jerry's!*" Heather shrieked, just as she did every Friday.

"Okay," I said again. "It's a long walk, though, honey."

"Ben-n-Jerry's," said Heather firmly. Heather already has her future mapped: she plans to marry either Ben or Jerry—precisely which ice cream entrepreneur is to be the lucky man hasn't been finalized yet—when she grows up to ensure a steady supply of premium ice cream. Heather, like all little girls, has her eye squarely fixed on the main chance.

And so we went to Ben and Jerry's ice cream parlor, where I had a strawberry sundae with vanilla ice cream and Heather had pistachio walnut with fudge and Reese's Pieces. There's nothing like a well-balanced diet for a growing girl. I consoled myself by thinking of what my mother would say if she could see us now.

After dinner, Heather and I walked slowly home, enjoying twilight and the passing parade. New York is a summer festival.

And that is pretty much how I spent the weekend: innocently indulging in modern family values. I vacuumed the apartment and took Heather to the library; I posed for Lizard, who had developed an urgent need for a tall model to portray a Wicked Queen; I read the latest Kinsey Millhone mystery.

Not once did I think about Dayborne Ventures or about my current temporary boss, Mr. J. Abercrombie Davis. I'm a temp; when I leave a job at five, *all* of me leaves. It's one reason I haven't had either an ulcer or a nervous breakdown yet.

And on Monday morning I dressed myself up as a sober member of the working public once more, dropped Heather off at MOP's day care center, and returned for another fun-filled week at beautiful Dayborne Ventures.

Chapter Two

Monday

When I arrived at my desk in Dayborne's offices on the twenty-first floor, I began the Monday-morning ritual of preparing for the day's work. I unlocked my desk and put my pocketbook in the lower right-hand drawer. I untied my Rockport Walkers, tucked them away under the desk, and slid on my plain black leather pumps. I turned on my computer and booted up the word processing system.

Since I prefer to arrive fifteen minutes early rather than fifteen seconds late, that day I was the second person to arrive at my momentary home base, Corporate Restructuring and Accounts. J. Abercrombie himself had arrived first. I knew this because his door was closed, which was the first thing Davis did in the morning when he came in. Well, the second thing. First he stalked past Fran—and me—without a word. *Then* he slammed the door to his office closed. This guy would never make it big in the user-friendly South.

Since there were no signs of life in my little corner of Dayborne heaven, I walked down past the ladies' room to the staff lounge to see if anyone had started the coffeemaker going yet.

Someone had; the rich dark scent of brewing Maxwell House filled the recycled air. I poured myself a cup, added milk and two packets of Sweet 'N Low, and tossed the empty pink envelopes into the trash on top of the blue foil Maxwell House packet.

INDIA EDGHILL

When I got back to my desk, Fran was at hers, hastily
stuffing her oversized pink plastic handbag into *her* lower
right-hand desk drawer.

"Hi," I said, and she jumped slightly and turned, hand
pressed to her plump bosom.

"Oh, it's you," she said on a half-gasp. "You gave me
quite a start."

Thinking I knew what she meant, I glanced over at the
polished teak door upon which an oval brass plaque announced in chaste italic script that "Mr. J. Abercrombie
Davis, Executive Vice President" resided within.

"Don't worry—his door's been closed, so no one'll know
you were—" I checked my watch, "—gee, all of sixty seconds late."

"I'm not late. I was in the ladies'. I *always* get here at
eight-thirty, you know. To make Mr. Davis's coffee. Just
like I did this morning. You know how particular he is." Although Fran only drank herb tea, she made coffee twice
daily for her boss in his own personal private coffeemaker,
which resided upon one end of the long mahogany credenza
in his office. Fran used Davis's own personal private coffee,
too—Maxwell House apparently wasn't good enough for
him. Myself, I don't care what the brand is as long as the
caffeine count is high.

"Sure," I said. Fran was chattering more than usual this
morning, and to be perfectly frank, I didn't listen with any
particular attention or sympathy. The woman seemed to be
perfectly happy with her eternal role as Davis's Doormat—
and as I knew only too well, it takes two to dance that particular dominance-submission waltz.

I ought to know. When I'd been married to Ravenal, I'd
had down all the steps by heart. Ravenal demanded; I
obeyed. Ravenal pleaded; I acquiesced. Ravenal apologized;

40

I forgave. See? Simple. Easy. Almost, in a sickening way, enjoyable.

At least you always know what you're supposed to be doing: Standing By Your Man. You get serious brownie points for that feat of endurance, where I come from.

The morning stalked by on leaden Monday feet. There was no word from Mr. Davis's office, so I efficiently answered phones, took messages, and typed two short memos. In between these tasks I enjoyed the passing parade of Dayborne Ventures; as the temp, the outsider, I could observe this particular patch of corporate jungle with the detached interest of the scientist.

A truly high-ticket firm, Dayborne Ventures was sleek in that heartless corporate fashion that negates all humanity. The ultra-modern corridors and offices were inhabited by men and women dressed for success in all the possible shades of gray, from ice to charcoal. These were the executives, the high-riders, the smooth-cruising sharks. Occasionally a maverick in something radical, like navy, slid by.

Secretaries flashed past, slim and quick in bright silk dresses. Everyone was obviously on his or her way to accomplish some task of overwhelming importance to the free world—or at least to Dayborne.

At ten the robot mail truck trundled slowly along its track through the corridor. As it rolled past my desk I got up and walked alongside the Dayborne R2D2 to collect the morning's mail from the bin marked "Davis/Corp. Res. & Accts." Which, translated from business-speak, meant, "Davis's Department: Corporate Restructuring and Accounts." Which does not, as far as I can tell, translate at all into plain English.

I opened and sorted the mail preparatory to handing the letters, memos, and other business ephemera to Fran for further analysis before they went before the critical gaze of Mr. Davis, Ex. V.P., Corp. Res. & Accts. The usual, the usual, the usual—and then I unfolded a letter and found myself staring at a sheet of plain white paper which bore the following message: "You won't get away with it."

After the first instant's freeze, I took a deep breath and a closer look. The words had been cut from a newspaper and taped to the paper. Careful not to touch any more of it than I already had, I turned it over; nothing. I held it up to the light; no watermarks. Setting it down with equal care, I examined the envelope: standard number ten (business size); first class stamp; postmarked at the main Manhattan Post Office the previous Wednesday. There's nothing like the prompt mail delivery in the Big Apple, thank God.

After playing Jessica Fletcher with the letter and envelope, I called, "Hey, Fran, better take a look at this."

"What?" Fran obligingly heaved herself out of her chair and walked over, reaching for the letter.

"Don't touch it," I said. "There may be fingerprints."

Fran leaned over and examined the letter closely. "Oh," she said after a moment, "another one. Don't worry about it, he gets lots of these." She scooped up letter and envelope before I could stop her. "I'll just file these with the others."

"Shouldn't we tell Mr. Davis?"

"Don't worry about it," Fran repeated. She hauled open one of her file drawers and dropped the hate mail into one of the Pendaflex files. Fran kept ferociously detailed files that she understandably hated anyone else to touch; I wondered what *that* folder was labeled.

"Did he ever call the police about it?" I asked.

"He's an important man; he gets lots of crank letters." Fran seemed almost proud of this rather dubious achievement.

Maybe, but I'd been there three weeks and hadn't seen any yet. Of course, maybe Fran had been intercepting the mail before I got it—no, that would be "going outside of proper channels." Executive secretaries did not chase after Robbie the Mail Truck. Ordinary secretaries like me—and Annabel Price, for whom I was substituting—did that.

As you can see, Dayborne favored a strict chain of command system. This efficient system ensured that everyone always had someone below them in the hierarchy to shoulder any blame that needed assigning.

And people wonder why I don't take a permanent job with one of these wonderful companies.

At 10:30 the refreshment wagon bell rang in the main lobby by the elevators; there was an instant exodus in that direction that reminded me of the Eloi answering the summons of the Morlocks. I admit I joined the inexorable flow towards caffeine and sugar myself, pausing only to ask if Fran wanted anything.

"Oh, no—" she glanced over her shoulder at the closed door to Davis's office.

"You sure? What about your traditional jelly doughnut?"

"Oh, yes. That would be lovely." She fumbled in her outsize purse for change and handed me a crumpled dollar bill.

"What about him?" I asked, indicating Davis's door with a tilt of my chin. He'd never wanted anything yet, but the habit of helpfulness dies hard.

"Oh, no—you know the rules. Mr. Davis is not to be disturbed unless he leaves *explicit* instructions." This was said in the reproachful tone of a kindergarten teacher who has been sadly disappointed in one's playground conduct.

"Fine," I said, and went off to procure and bring back one cellophane-wrapped jelly doughnut for Fran and one

Coca-Cola for me. Classic, of course. As my mother always says, "If you can't say something nice, don't say anything at all," and so of New Coke, I prefer to say absolutely nothing.

The rest of the morning passed quietly, all ninety minutes of it. Then it was noon, and lunchtime.

I sat on a concrete bench in the little pedestrian plaza outside the building while I ate my sandwich, and then walked across the street to Battery Park. I always felt that New York Harbor provided a pleasant contrast to the concrete canyons of the financial district.

Especially on such a glorious June summer-hot day, when the sky was a smooth pale blue and sun sparkles danced diamond-bright across the dark green-green surface of the harbor. Out in the harbor, the Statue of Liberty lifted her lamp. Past her, in the middle distance, the ferry chugged its industrious way towards Staten Island. Overhead seagulls whirled and screamed. The wind off the water tugged at my neatly pinned hair and teased the hem of my skirt.

Walking at the water's edge made me feel wild and free; it was worth having to take ten minutes at the other end of my lunch hour to disappear into the ladies' room and re-tidy myself into Mrs. Upshaw, Perfect Secretary.

When I returned to my desk at one, Fran was brushing crumbs from her desk into the wastebasket. The Davis door was still closed.

"You should get out at lunch," I told Fran. "It's good for you." Fran, as far as I could tell, never left her desk at all during the day if she could help it.

"Oh, no—*he* might need me."

"Obi-wan Kenobi?" I muttered, sliding into my secretarial chair.

"What?" Fran said blankly.

"Nothing," I said. "By the way, are you sure he's in there?"

"Oh, yes—there's nothing on his calendar, you see, and he would certainly have *called* me if anything had prevented him from coming in, and—"

I stopped really listening, and began typing in new numbers on an old spreadsheet.

And if you say I should have been more suspicious at the time, all I can say is you haven't worked in as many offices as I have.

For example, you probably haven't worked in the office where the boss's secretary does nothing but answer the phone and knit her afghan. Doing my world-famous imitation of Sherlock Holmes, I deduced this when I opened her desk drawers to discover balls of wool, knitting needles, and a half-finished orange and green afghan taking up the space usually filled by file folders and office supplies.

Or in the office where the boss leaves for lunch at 11:50, announcing he'll be back in an hour, and doesn't return until the next morning at 9:00. The first day I worked that job, I nearly called the police when—oh, let's call him Mr. X—didn't return by 3:00. When I finally went to tell the office manager that X hadn't come back yet, she just laughed.

Or in the office where the boss hangs around your desk most of the day chatting about sports, movies, and his military service. This last chap then wonders why nothing ever seems to get done on time in his office. And he's serious, too.

Or in the many, many offices where they simply don't trust a temporary secretary to be able to do more than keep the regular employee's chair warm until she returns. This is very boring.

Important Safety Tip for the professional temp: Always Bring a Book.

It's also a good idea to bring along your personal correspondence. Letter writing enables you to look terribly industrious without endangering the esoteric filing system that no one but Valerie-on-Vacation can either understand or negotiate.

At 2:45, Fran cast me an agonized glance and murmured that she really must . . . She trailed this statement off with a delicacy of feeling that my mother would have admired; I assured Fran that her secret was safe with me and that I'd hold Fort Zinderneuf in the face of all comers until her return.

"What?" said Fran.

"Go ahead," I told her. "You need a break. Oh—if you hear the 3:00 bell, would you be kind enough to get me a Coke?"

"I won't be that long," she assured me, and hastened down the hall to the ladies' room, clutching her big pink purse.

Shaking my head, I returned to my spreadsheet. Less than five minutes later, I heard knocking and looked up to see Raymond Clough tapping on Mr. Davis's closed door. This was lamentably contrary to Dayborne procedure; all approaches to a Great Man—or Great Woman—must be made via his or her secretary. Chain of command, you know.

"Excuse me," I said, "may I help you?"

"I hope so. I need to talk to Davis. New info on the RE&T merger; he's got to know about it ASAP." Mr. Clough worked down in the far corner of the twenty-first floor, doing something in Overseas Investment Futures. Moderately tall, moderately dark, and moderately handsome, he looked amazingly similar to all the other Dayborne Assistant Vice Presidents. Idly, I wondered if Dayborne cut out their AVPs with cookie cutters and then used some different colored icings to achieve the illusion of variety.

"I'm sorry," I said. "Mr. Davis can't be disturbed if his door's closed."

"Damn it—" Clough began, and then stopped. After a moment, he said, "Where's Fran?"

"Ladies'," I said. "But she said—"

"Look, can't you at least buzz his intercom and get him to answer his damn phone?"

If I'd been a Dayborne employee, I might have hesitated more; Davis's lousy temper was notorious. But I wasn't employed by Dayborne, but by MOP, and if any place gave me enough grief, I'd pick up my marbles and go home. And I'd have a new temp assignment the next day, if I wanted one. Once I'd even had a new one that same afternoon, but that was a special case involving long-standing and especially desperate MOP clients.

And while it was possible that Davis had spoken to Fran (who wouldn't bother to tell me, and why should she?), or had popped out while I was away from my desk, it was also possible that the guy was lying in there incapacitated by a heart attack or a stroke. (His blood pressure had to be about 300 over 190, minimum.)

"Okay, I'll buzz him," I told Raymond Clough, and pushed the intercom button. And held it down, waiting. Although the walls and doors at Dayborne were as rock-solid as its financial status, I heard a faint irritating drone inside Davis's office. I admit I was listening pretty hard, though.

After a solid ninety seconds, I looked at Clough. "He's not answering. Look—I think we should go on in there. He may need help."

47

I thought I heard Clough mutter something that sounded suspiciously like, "He sure does," but I pretended I hadn't heard and we both headed for the door. I tried the knob and discovered the door was locked just about the time Fran came scuttling back, breathing hard.

"Cornelia! What are you doing? Mr. Davis will be *furious* if he's interrupted—"

"He'll be a sight more furious if he's had a stroke and is lying there without the strength to call 911," I said. I was starting to wonder if Davis was even in there. Maybe he'd snuck out while we weren't looking. Maybe he'd suddenly wanted to spend the afternoon with his secret mistress, or at the movies, or at a bar, without informing the ever-vigilant, ever-concerned Fran.

"Right," said Clough, and tried to turn the knob he'd just watched me fail to turn. Perhaps he thought it would miraculously unlock under a masculine touch.

However, the locked door was admirably gender-neutral; in other words, it was just as locked for Raymond Clough, AVP, as it was for Cornelia Upshaw, temporary secretary.

So Clough knocked again—pounded, rather. "Davis! You in there?"

"Oh, no; oh, dear—" Fran was literally wringing her hands in distress. "You don't think—"

"I think," I said over Clough's continued pounding, "that you'd better get someone to open that door. Hey, Fran, don't you have a key to his office?"

Fran stared at me wide-eyed, as if I'd suggested multiple orgies in the lobby. "Well, yes, but Mr. Davis said to *never*—"

"This is an emergency," I announced firmly. "Come on, Fran, get the key. Everybody's looking," I added as the final inducement to compliance. Heads were turning as people

48

walked past; other heads were poking out of offices. Nobody, I noticed, did anything so sensible as come over and ask what was going on, or if we needed any help.

To a steady stream of "Oh, dears," Fran rummaged in her purse and produced a veritable handful of keys. The key to her boss's office door was obvious—it was the one attached to a large enameled tag that said "VIP." It was also the one that fell to the floor while Fran was fumbling about sorting semi-identical keys.

I scooped up the key before Fran's worser sense came to the fore again and slid it into the keyhole of J. Abercrombie Davis's locked door. Then I turned the key, and turned the knob, and opened the door. And then I walked into J. Abercrombie Davis's office.

He was slumped over his desk, and he was dead. I knew that with a sure clarity that surprised me; until that moment, I hadn't known that the dead resemble the sleeping living only as much as a photograph does.

Even though I was positive that he was dead, I still forced myself to walk over to his desk. I was also sure it was too late to revive him, even with modern technology. That office was empty; the occupant gone. But like a good citizen, I went over to try and check for a pulse, or respiration.

I touched the back of his hand. The flesh was cool, inelastic. No longer human. Beside that inanimate hand rested a cream ceramic mug that stated "BOSS" in large brown letters. I bet Fran had given it to him one Christmas. He must have been lying dead across his desk all day, and we'd all been going back and forth and never known—

It was a lonely way to die. Swallowing hard, I backed away from the desk and turned to face Raymond Clough and Fran Jenkins.

"He's dead," I said. "I—I guess somebody better call 911."

Death isn't neat, especially sudden death. I'd expected somebody to faint; I hadn't thought it would be Raymond Clough. But one look at the body and the poor man keeled right over. I ran one way to get some water and Fran ran the other to stare down at her ex-boss.

On my way to the staff room, I also grabbed the first person in even semi-authority I saw. Someone had to take charge, and it needed to be someone Dayborne. Since Harriet Benson was the first AVP I saw, she was the winner of the day's No Prize.

"Oh, thank goodness," I said, as she came out the ladies' room door just as I reached it. "Would you mind going along to Mr. Davis's office? He's—"

"Tell him I'll have the damned Anson report to him in five minutes," Harriet clipped back, and I had to block her path to keep her from rushing off report-wards.

"Harriet, he's dead," I said, as gently as it's ever possible to say words like that. When she just stared at me, I repeated the words, equally gently, and explained how Clough and Fran and I had come to defy Dayborne Tradition and open Davis's office door. I'm still not sure whether Harriet Benson was more shocked by my announcement that Davis was dead or by my admission that we'd opened his door without his permission.

"Are you sure he'd dead?" Harriet asked at last, and I just nodded. "I'd better come and check," she said, but she waited until I went into the ladies' room and filled my hands with wet paper towels, and then followed me back down the hall to Davis's office.

When we got there, Clough was sitting up (he'd turned an interesting shade of pale putty-greige) and Fran had pulled herself together enough to make the necessary phone call.

"They—they said they'd be here as soon as they can." That said, Fran began weeping silently but copiously; I tried to put an arm around her, but she shook me off and began wandering around the office. As if on some sort of secretarial autopilot, she began straightening the papers Davis's forward slump over his desk had disarranged. Then she picked up the half-empty coffee mug and stared into it disconsolately.

"Fran, honey, it was probably a heart attack," I said. "He obviously didn't suffer any."

"Too bad," snapped Harriet Benson—obviously before she remembered that Davis was now dead, and no longer fair game. "I mean—Cornelia's right, Fran; it's better this way."

Fortunately, she shut up then and didn't elaborate on this statement. Fran only shook her head, and took away a file of papers and the coffee mug. Tidy to the last.

The paramedics showed up in their own sweet time— reasonable enough, as there was nothing left to do for Davis but bury him—but highly irritating to those of us with things to do and places to be. By four, the Dayborne staff like Harriet Benson and Raymond Clough had decided waiting for the paramedics wasn't in their job description, and by 4:30 the other sympathetic and curious on-lookers (I'd shut the door to the office, but the door itself became an object of major interest) had all drifted off.

The hands of the clock were inching on towards 5:00, and I had to go pick up Heather and my dry-cleaning. Not only were there no paramedics in sight, but Fran had already cleaned everything cleanable, tidied everything else, and was reciting a positively Shakespearean eulogy to the late Mr. Davis.

"He was always such a *good* man—treated me so wonderfully—never a cross word—"

Absently, I wondered how Fran could possibly believe the pious pap she was spouting. If I'd learned one thing in my misspent youth, it was that death didn't improve the character any. I snuck a glance at my watch; 4:46. "Uh, look, Fran—"

"Such an *appreciative* boss—not like some of them, you know? Why, he always said no one else could make coffee the way I did it—you know, he said he could tell right off if I hadn't made it—"

"Um-hum," I responded vaguely. "Look, Fran, I—"

"Oh, dear, you're right. I—I'd better check his office and finish straightening up—you know he can't stand an untidy desk—" Here more tears choked off her voice. Wiping her eyes again, Fran jumped up, grateful to have thought of one last task to do for the Dear Departed.

"Fran," I said gently, "I think you'd better just sit down. Okay?"

"Oh, but—"

"His office is fine," I assured her; I didn't add that Davis ought to be past caring what his office looked like now. "And you already straightened it up, remember? Just leave it alone now, honey."

Just about then, the paramedics arrived. Finally. Fortunately, they had very little interest in me; I directed them to Fran and the body of Mr. Davis, in that order, and fled the premises.

I was even on time to pick up Heather *and* get my drycleaning. And I'm afraid the untimely death of J. Abercrombie Davis, EVP, didn't exactly prey upon my mind. It wasn't, after all, as if I'd either known the man well or liked him at all. I'd only worked for him, temporarily, for three weeks.

As I recall, the recitation of My Day At the Office to my sister Lizard went something as follows:

Me (casually): "My boss at Dayborne died today, and nobody noticed."

Lizard (pretending to care): "Oh, yeah? How come?"

Me: "Heart attack, and he was such a control freak he always kept the door closed and screamed bloody murder at anyone who opened it without his express permission. So his door was closed, and nobody checked all day."

Lizard: "Some great control, huh? So what's for dinner?"

Me (very bland): "Meat loaf."

Lizard (outraged, but if *she* won't cook, she's got to put up with it): "*Again?*"

CHAPTER THREE

TUESDAY MORNING

Tuesday started normally; I arrived at Dayborne at the usual time, because although I wondered what I was doing at Dayborne now my boss-of-the-moment was dead, nobody had called me to cancel the job. So here I dutifully was.

Fran was already seated at her desk. Instead of one of her usual bright polyester suits or dresses in some cheerfully out-of-date color like shocking pink or tropical orange, she was wearing a plain black suit, its jacket buttoned up to the neck. Her eyes were red from crying and puffy from being rubbed.

"Oh. Cornelia. I'm glad you're here. It's been—" Fran scrubbed at her already abused eyes again with a sodden Kleenex.

"Well, nobody said not to come, so I assumed I still had a job here," I said. "Look, Fran, maybe you should go on home? Or go lie down?" Her grief was so uncontrollable that she seemed more like a bereft widow than a suddenly bossless secretary.

"Oh, I can't. There's so much to do. The whole department relied on us—on Mr. Davis." Her mouth trembled; she pressed her lips firmly together.

I wanted to ask who was going to take over the department now, but the question seemed unkind, somehow. So I simply nodded, and settled myself at my own desk and held myself in readiness for whatever work might cross my path.

The department head's death seemed to have caused an excited panic among the lesser vice presidents he'd controlled; a sort of subdued feeding frenzy as they all dashed in seeking memos, letters, and files from his office. At first Fran had tried to prevent this defilement of Davis's office, but with him dead, she had been abruptly demoted from Guardian of the Gate to the Invisible Woman.

"Look," one particularly shark-like Junior VP said, in response to Fran's statement that Mr. Davis didn't want the Africa files moved, "Davis is dead. Who cares what he wants?"

That was the point at which Fran disappeared into the ladies' room, probably to cry her eyes out in private, and I decided I needed caffeine now, not when the mid-morning snack cart came by. I locked my desk and went down the hall to the staff room just in time to see Harriet Benson drop her coffee cup and start gasping like a startled goldfish. A second later she was lying in the pool of coffee spreading over the carpet and I was kneeling beside her holding her hands. Her fingers spasmed around mine hard enough to grind my hand's bones together.

"Harriet, say something, can you talk?" For at first, you see, I thought she might have caught something in her throat, and as long as a person can talk, the airway isn't blocked. And you don't have to try the Heimlich maneuver.

"Can't breathe," Harriet whispered. Her skin was fading, graying; I pried my hands out of hers and grabbed the staff room phone and called Security, and then called 911. Then I put my arms around Harriet Benson and held her, and stared at the dark stain of spilled coffee surrounding us.

With a life to save, rather than a dead body to remove,

the paramedics arrived within minutes—ten very long minutes during which a security guard arrived and kept Harriet alive with mouth-to-mouth resuscitation. Even as they asked swift questions about what had happened, the paramedics slapped an oxygen mask over Harriet's nose and mouth.

Of course, I couldn't answer any of their urgent queries. No, I didn't know if the victim was asthmatic, allergic, anemic. All I knew was that I'd walked in just as she'd suffered the attack of whatever-it-was. And at the very last minute, as the paramedics wheeled the gurney out with Harriet strapped to it and hooked up to the oxygen tank, I caught up her fallen coffee cup.

"She was drinking this—maybe she had a reaction to—" Before I could finish my half-formed thought that Harriet might suddenly have turned allergic to artificial sweetener, one of the paramedics snatched the cup and tossed it into a plastic bag.

"Yeah, maybe, thanks lady, doctor'll check." With that, paramedics, patient, and security guard whipped off down the corridor towards the elevators.

"People come and go so quickly here," I said, and then looked down at my skirt, which had large coffee-colored blotches on it. I'd have to either go home and change, go out and buy a new skirt at the closest store, or pretend that tie-dye was back as a fashion statement. As I walked back to my desk, trying to decide which option was least trouble, I for once was glad that Dayborne employees had so little curiosity about anything beyond their own cubicles. Despite the second arrival of paramedics in twenty-four hours, the halls of Dayborne were clear and quiet. No one cared, as long as whatever had happened didn't affect his or her own department's bottom line.

At least I didn't have to explain what had happened a dozen times before I got back to my own work area. I did tell Fran, who merely stared at me, and then picked up her phone.

"Amber? Please tell maintenance the twenty-first floor staff room needs cleaning immediately." Fran set down the receiver and regarded me a bit reproachfully. "You have coffee stains on your skirt," she said.

I considered and rejected several stinging rejoinders; Fran's eyes were even redder and puffier than they'd been when I first saw her that morning. The poor thing plainly barely knew what she was saying. "Yes, I know. I'm trying to decide whether to go home and change or not. Can you manage by yourself if I take an extra-long lunch hour?"

"Of course." This was said with a certain pride; Frances Jenkins could and would manage to cope as long as necessary.

I smiled. "Okay, then, why don't I leave now? If I can't find a skirt over at Labels for Less, I'll run home and change."

"I suppose you'll have to; you can't work here wearing that."

Again I bit back the words I wanted to say—after all, not only was Fran emotionally fragile, she had a certain point. And I didn't want to spend the rest of the day explaining why I had brown blotches on my skirt. I unlocked my desk drawer, took out my pocketbook, and went off in search of a suitable replacement for my ruined garment.

Over at Labels for Less, I found a perfectly charming skirt—corn-yellow rayon splashed with brilliant poppies— and wore it back to Dayborne. It was flashier than my usual work attire, but I liked it and it coordinated well enough with my cream suit jacket. Then I finished my lunch break with a long walk along the water's edge at Battery Park. Somehow, after the morning's crisis, I needed a lot of fresh air.

CHAPTER FOUR

WEDNESDAY MORNING

In certain cases, the police can be as prompt as the paramedics. When I arrived at Dayborne Ventures at 8:45 on Wednesday morning the place was crawling with them.

Or so Amber the twenty-first floor receptionist told me, with a meaningful glance at the one (count him, one) youthful lad in blue who was standing around looking both stern and sheepish. In fact, he'd opened and held the door for me, and called me "ma'am"; a perfect darling and fortunately way too young for me. The police, Amber added in a low, husky whisper better suited to the retailing of erotic state secrets, were Here About Mr. Davis.

"What about him?" I asked.

"They think he was *murdered*," Amber hissed dramatically, with an even more meaningful glance at the cop at the door.

"What? But I thought it was a heart attack."

Amber shrugged; three pairs of gold earrings flashed. "All I know is the place is just *crawling* with cops and, boy, is Management pissed off. Thought you'd like to know."

Well, it's always a good idea to know when Management's throwing a hissy-fit, but, "Why me, particularly?"

"Well, honey," said Amber sweetly, "you found the body, didn't you? Doesn't that make you the number one suspect?" She regarded me avidly; was she going to be able to sell her story to *Sixty Minutes* or the *National Enquirer*?

"Wrong," I said, "the person who finds the body is *never* the one who did it. First rule of mystery writing."

"Yeah, well what about that Roger Ackroyd case you told me about?"

"Amber," I explained patiently, "that was a *novel*. It didn't really happen. Look, I've got to get to my desk while I've still got a job here."

"Well, all I've got to say is there're plenty of people here who'd've been happy to bash that guy's head in. Look, do you think this will be in the *Daily News*?"

"Lord, I certainly hope not," I said. "Look, just buzz me in, will you? I'm almost late."

As a Charleston girl with a regional reputation to live down, I pride myself on promptness. It was now 8:55; as I said, almost late.

I got to my desk promptly at 8:59 and observed that Mr. Davis's door was now crisscrossed by two bands of yellow-and-black striped tape. In the center, just below the brass name plaque, was a large white sign that stated, "Police Barricade: Do Not Cross." Apparently Amber had been right—at least about the police being here, anyway.

I looked from the door to Fran. "What's going on? Oh, and how's Harriet?" Oddly enough, at that moment I did not connect Davis's death with Harriet's sudden collapse.

"I don't know. Nobody will tell me anything. Rummaging through Mr. Davis's office like vultures—and now the *police*—they're talking to everybody. They say Mr. Davis was *murdered*." Bewilderment colored Fran's unsteady voice. "Who would want to murder Mr. Davis?"

The words "practically anyone who knew him" sprang instantly to mind; I didn't speak them. "Well, I'm sure the police will find out. Look, are you sure you're okay? Maybe a cup of coffee?"

"Oh, I *never* drink coffee. It's so bad for you—all that caffeine. I tried to get Mr. Davis to switch to herb tea, but—" Her soft face crumpled under a fresh attack of grief. "Oh, what am I going to do? I've *always* been Mr. Davis's secretary. Why, he didn't know how to manage without me."

Which was as good an epitaph for their relationship as any. Guiltily aware that my emotions were totally uninvolved, I went over to pat Fran's shoulder. "It's just purely awful, honey, but you've got to pull yourself together. There's—there's that quarterly report to get out, you know. And you're a terrific secretary—you'll get a new job in no time."

Fran lifted her head and regarded me almost balefully. "In today's job market? At my age?" Suddenly her voice was harsh, almost hostile. "All they want these days is size eights with lots of hair and a pretty face—they don't care if you can type, or file, or even if you know the alphabet—" Abruptly her voice wavered back to "unhappy little girl" again. "And I've *never* worked for anyone else; he hired me when I was fresh out of business school."

I bit my lip; I couldn't think, at the moment, of anything else either true or comforting to say. Fortunately, I didn't have to, because another stalwart member of the New York City Police Department strode up to us and requested the presence of Ms. Jenkins in the conference room.

"I'll be right there." Fran blew her nose rather defiantly and hauled a handful of fresh Kleenex out of the box on her desk. "And I guess you're right, Cornelia—can you manage on the quarterly while I'm gone?"

I assured her I could, and watched her walk down the

hall beside the policeman, and felt sorry for her.

Because Fran was right—she was fifty-plus and a one-boss girl (and I use this non-politically-correct term intentionally). In today's job market all her secretarial expertise wouldn't weigh much in the balance against her age and her looks. Maybe she could temp, but she didn't strike me as the temping sort.

In a sense, Fran Jenkins had just been widowed; now the only person she could depend upon was herself. I remembered what a shock sudden widowhood was, although I'd at least been spared the agony of grief—or of sudden poverty. Still, Fran struck me as a saver. For her sake, I just hoped Fran had kept her personal finances as tidy as she'd always kept her boss's office and files.

While Fran was away I dutifully worked on the quarterly report—or tried to. I actually didn't have time to do much typing; the phone rang approximately every ninety seconds, as if everyone in the corporate world felt the need to call and verify the news of J. Abercrombie's demise. I spent my time explaining that yes, Mr. Davis was dead, and no, I didn't know anything else about it, and yes, Fran was here, but no, she wasn't at her desk, and yes, the quarterly reports were still being produced on schedule and I'd have her call the caller back. I was relieved when Fran finally returned, looking even redder around the eyes than she had before.

"They want to see you now," she said, and collapsed into her chair.

I got up, handed her a stack of phone message slips an inch thick, and went rather gratefully off to the conference room. While I was truly sorry for Fran, I now have only a limited tolerance for rampaging emotionalism. At least the police wouldn't burst into tears every three minutes.

And I'd never been questioned by the police before. I was sure it would be interesting to compare truth with crime fiction.

The main conference room at Dayborne occupies the center of the twentieth floor and is larger than the average Manhattan apartment. The walls are polished tiger oak; the lights are overhead and indirect. A long sweep of highly expensive, aerodynamically curved table occupies the center of the room. Like a casino, or an operating room, or any other place in which you are supposed to forget time and common sense, there are no windows.

This undoubtedly made the conference room an eminently suitable location for the police to question suspects.

Not certain what to expect, I went through the door another nice young policeman opened for me and paused. The conference room was not swarming with cops; at the far end of the table two men sat, papers and Styrofoam coffee cups in front of them. One slender black man, one large white one; both wearing plain ordinary civilian clothes.

As I balanced on the threshold like an undecided cat, both men rose to their feet.

"Mrs. Upshaw?" The white policeman—at least, I assumed the men were both policemen—asked. When I nodded, he smiled. "I'm Lieutenant Kosciusko, and this is Detective Morton. Would you mind sitting down? We'd like to ask you a few questions."

"Of course," I said. What would they have said if I *had* minded sitting down?

As I walked down along the seemingly endless curve of the conference table towards them, I suddenly found myself regarding Lieutenant Kosciusko with an appraising interest

that startled me. After an intensive course of home study—
my marriage—I had sworn off men.

Of course, to be absolutely fair, I hadn't been married to
a man. As I'd learned too late, I'd been married to a boy, an
eternal Reckless Golden Youth who'd made Peter Pan look
mature in comparison.

Lieutenant Kosciusko didn't look even remotely boyish,
and certainly not reckless, being tall and broad; big in a
massive, solid fashion. He had pale red hair that gleamed
copper under the overhead lights. Since I have a literary
mind, he instantly reminded me of Merton Heimrich, the
State Police captain in the Lockridge mysteries. For a
fleeting instant I wondered if Lieutenant Kosciusko, too,
thought of his large self as a hippopotamus . . .

"Just have a seat," he said, smiling again. Fine lines
around his eyes tilted upwards when he smiled. "We'll try
not to keep you too long."

I assured him that that was quite all right, and we all sat
down. I made sure I sat carefully, like a lady, and folded my
hands on my lap. "I'm glad to help, truly I am."

Detective Morton glanced over at me. "From the South,
Mrs. Upshaw?" He was medium brown and dapper, more
smartly dressed than Lieutenant Kosciusko. I wondered,
briefly, what prejudices Detective Morton held against
Southerners.

"Originally," I said. "Usually it doesn't show." Over the
past few years, I'd worked hard to lose the accent and
achieve a professional neutrality. As Detective Morton had
just noted, I hadn't completely succeeded.

"You're probably a bit nervous at being questioned by
the police," he informed me kindly. "But there's nothing to
be nervous about; we just need to ask you some simple
questions—" He paused; glanced at Lieutenant Kosciusko,

who nodded. "Would you like some coffee? Tea?"

"Is that one of the simple questions?" I asked, and they both smiled.

"No," said Kosciusko, "we're just trying to put you at ease, Mrs. Upshaw—" He paused, continued after a beat, "It's 'Mrs.'?"

"That's right," I said. I use the full title of a married woman, rather than the noncommittal "Ms." I earned it, and its usage keeps away a number of pests, even these days.

"You're divorced?"

"Widowed," I told him; I don't usually bother to mention this fact, but as I told myself virtuously, you have to tell policemen the truth, however irrelevant.

"Oh," he said, and then, gently, "I'm sorry." He even looked sorry.

"Don't be." This was a little too blunt, perhaps, but I didn't want him feeling guilty for upsetting a lady who wasn't in the least distressed. I found myself sneaking a glance at his left hand. No ring. But these days that doesn't necessarily mean much.

For the first time I wished I weren't still wearing Ravenal's ring, but slipping my wedding ring off now would be just too tacky for words. And Lieutenant Kosciusko was a professional detective; they probably notice little things like that.

"All right," the lieutenant said, after a moment's pause. "Let's get started, then. Charlie?"

Detective Morton picked up a sheet of paper and peered at it. "Um—you're not on the employee list, Mrs. Upshaw. New here?"

"No," I said. "I'm a temp—a temporary employee hired to fill in."

"Companies do that much?"

"A lot. People go on vacation, or maternity leave. Or quit suddenly, and they need someone until they hire the new person. And a lot of companies hire temps instead of permanent employees—that way they don't have to pay any benefits. So it's really cheaper for them."

"So you've been here—"

"Three weeks," I said. "I'm supposed to be here for six, while, while Annabel Price—that's the assistant secretary—has her baby and some maternity leave."

"Okay," said Detective Morton, with another glance at Lieutenant Kosciusko. "Now tell us about Monday."

So I did. I started with my arrival at Dayborne at 8:45 a.m. and continued straight on through until the arrival of the paramedics at 4:55 p.m. It didn't take very long; it's truly amazing how little actually happens in the average eight-hour day in an office.

"And then the paramedics came, and I went home," I finished.

"Why the hurry to leave, Mrs. Upshaw?" Detective Morton again; apparently he'd gotten tapped for "bad cop" today. Mystery novels are good for something besides putting you to sleep, after all.

"Because it was almost five and I wanted to get my daughter from day care and pick up my dry-cleaning before the cleaners closed. I know that sounds awfully trivial, considering Mr. Davis was actually murdered. But I didn't know that at the time—and I'd *still* have had to pick up my daughter and the dry-cleaning, even if I *had* known."

Kosciusko and Detective Morton looked at each other again; Morton shook his head ruefully and Kosciusko smiled again. He had a nice smile.

"The living take precedence," he said. "I'm not so sure

about the dry-cleaning, though. Is there anything else you can tell us? Anyone who, oh, who might have held a grudge against Davis, say?"

"Practically anyone he worked with," I said. "Dayborne's in a cut-throat business."

"Uh, what does Dayborne *do,* exactly?" asked Detective Morton, leaning forward slightly, alert as a greyhound.

He actually sounded interested, so I smiled and said, "I'm not sure, but it's *very* competitive. The executives like to have shouting matches in the main hallways. The vice president with the loudest voice gets the biggest office," I finished.

Kosciusko leaned back; the chair, built for executives kept lean on a diet of eighty-hour weeks and black coffee, creaked alarmingly. He straightened hastily. "Now, what about that anonymous letter you say he received?"

"Did receive," I corrected.

"Did receive," Lieutenant Kosciusko echoed meekly; I thought I saw a glint of amusement in his hazel eyes.

"I told you," I said. "I gave it to his secretary Fran—Ms. Jenkins; she filed it. She said he gets lots of mail like that. In fact, she had a whole file folder full of it."

"I see," Kosciusko said. He looked to Morton, who shrugged and shook his head; no more questions from him, apparently. I expected to be politely dismissed—but then Lieutenant Kosciusko said, "All right, Mrs. Upshaw, now tell us about yesterday."

"Yesterday?" I said rather blankly. Then a rather horrifying light dawned. "Harriet Benson—is she—"

"She's still alive," Kosciusko said, "and thank you for the coffee, by the way."

"The coffee—" Then I remembered shoving Harriet's coffee cup at the paramedics; you didn't have to be

Sherlock Holmes to make the obvious deduction. "You mean somebody poisoned them? With coffee?"

Detective Morton regarded me sternly. "Why do you say that, Mrs. Upshaw?"

"Because I'm not an idiot, Detective Morton," I said, and Lieutenant Kosciusko smiled.

"No, you're not. And it's thanks to you that we had the coffee cup to analyze at all. So Ms. Benson is being treated for cyanide poisoning and will probably be fine."

"Cyanide? But isn't that always fatal?"

"There was only a trace, and she hadn't drunk much of it before a reaction set in."

But there must have been more than a trace in Davis's coffee, because Davis had died. Now, who would want to kill both J. Abercrombie Davis *and* Harriet Benson—? Suddenly the room seemed very cold, as if the air conditioning had kicked into overdrive. "Is this like the Tylenol poisonings?" I asked. The notorious unsolved Tylenol case, in which cyanide-laced Tylenol had killed seven people, totally at random. "Are you analyzing all the coffee?"

"We're working on it," Detective Morton said.

I hoped that Dayborne was buying a fresh stock of coffee. "I think I'll stick to tea for a while," I said—and promptly wondered if the cyanide could be in the water, or the milk, or the sugar, instead of in the coffee. Maybe I'd stick to cans of Coke . . .

At this point, the lieutenant gently reminded me that they wanted to know all about Tuesday, so I rallied my thoughts back into something approaching order. "Well, nobody called to cancel my job here, so on Tuesday, I got here at the usual time," I began, and told them all about Tuesday. I stopped after seeing the paramedics off, but both of the Nice Friendly Policemen professed great interest in the rest of my day as well, so I also told them all about buying a new skirt, eating lunch, walking along Battery Park, and spending all afternoon faxing a 150-page report to Dayborne's offices in Singapore, Bombay, and Capetown.

At last I stopped, waiting for further questions, but apparently I'd managed to bore not only myself, but New York's Finest, because all Lieutenant Kosciusko said was, "Well, that seems to be it—for now," he added. "If you think of anything else, give me a call at Homicide South. Here's my card—" His fingers brushed mine as he handed over a business card; oddly flustered, I managed to drop it; we both ducked for the card and narrowly missed banging our heads together.

In the process the card flipped under the table somewhere. Rather than crawl after it, Lieutenant Kosciusko pulled another one out of his pocket. By now he looked rather flushed; men hate to look ridiculous. (Come to that, *I* hate to look ridiculous, too—but I've learned that it won't kill me.)

"As I was saying," he went on rather grimly, "call me if you think of anything, or if anything comes up."

This time the card was handed over without incident; we both held only the outer edges of the card during the transfer. "Of course," I said.

Although I couldn't imagine what might come up; I'm not Nancy Drew, and the murderer was hardly apt to fling himself at me and suddenly Confess All.

"Oh, by the way—"

I was halfway to the door; I turned, wondering if this was the famous "Lieutenant Columbo" routine of the last-minute-yet-utterly-vital question, and if so, why Kosciusko was using the technique on me. I could hardly be a suspect—well, not a serious one, anyway.

"Did you ever meet Davis's wife? She ever come to the office?" Kosciusko asked.

Faintly surprised, I nodded. "Once. She came by last week to meet him for dinner and a show."

"And she was here Friday, wasn't she?" Detective Morton demanded.

"Oh," I said, surprised. I'd half-forgotten Brittany's Friday calls, but I guessed that the super-organized Fran hadn't; she'd probably logged each call in the message book, too. "No, Brittany—Mrs. Davis—wasn't here—not really. She just called up from the downstairs main lobby. They—she and her husband—were supposed to go somewhere, but he was running late. So she decided not to wait for him."

"I see," Lieutenant Kosciusko said; I wondered what it was he saw. "Did they get on well, do you know? Mr. and Mrs. Davis, that is?"

"She's a lot younger than he was," Detective Morton cut in, offering me the chance to agree, and to add criticisms of Brittany Davis, if I liked. I didn't.

"I don't really know how well they got on," I said carefully. "But I've only been here for three weeks. If you want to know about her, you should talk to Fran Jenkins again. She knows everything about Davis's life." She ought to; she managed most of it.

"Oh, we will," said Detective Morton.

Detective Kosciusko said, "Thank you, Mrs. Upshaw. You've been very helpful."

I doubted it, but that seemed to be that; I was dismissed.

Outside the conference room an Assistant Vice President named Carolyn Eaton waited, glaring at the policeman on guard and tapping the toe of her precisely-right work pump impatiently. "This *is* ridiculous. I have *work* to do." Carolyn's tone indicated it wasn't the first time she'd mentioned this. But apparently a Dayborne AVP didn't impress a member of the NYPD; in the duel of initials, his carried more clout.

"Okay, ma'am," he told Carolyn as I came out. "You can go in now."

"Well, it's about time," she snarled, brushing past him with the innate gentle courtesy that was the Dayborne executive's hallmark.

I smiled commiseratingly at the policeman—fellow peons sticking together—and started back through the corridor labyrinth towards my desk. Around the first corner I stopped and looked at the business card Lieutenant Kosciusko had given me.

His first name was Victor.

Of course, by the time I got back to my desk I was mentally kicking myself for acting like a flutter-headed moron. Why, I'd been so entranced by a pair of large, capable-looking hands and a pair of laugh-lined hazel eyes that I hadn't even asked what had killed Abercrombie Davis. I'd just assumed it was cyanide, but now I realized neither policeman had said any such thing. In fact, I was so cross with myself that I made the mistake of asking Fran how Davis had been killed.

I was sorry less than a minute later, and not only because it was a thoughtlessly cruel question.

Fran looked at me, and her eyes widened, and her face crumpled, and she began to cry again, and this time she didn't stop. Tears crescendoed into full-blown hysterics; I hauled her into the ladies' room, splashed water on her face, and left her there sitting on the mauve tiled floor while

I went and found the nearest Dayborne executive. To whom I explained in great detail that Ms. Jenkins was kind of upset about the whole murder thing. Appalled, he agreed that Ms. Jenkins should take the rest of the day off and go home.

Which is how I found myself riding out to the nether depths of Brooklyn with a faintly-sobbing Fran in a taxi paid for by Dayborne. Which was also, whether Dayborne knew it or not, paying for my time, too. MOP doesn't care whether its temps are typing or twiddling their thumbs or babysitting hysterical secretaries; MOP bills strictly by the hour.

I know it's clichéd to say it, but it really seemed to take forever to get to Fran's place. And when we did, I had no idea where we were. I live in the city—in Manhattan. Brooklyn was *terra incognita;* a seemingly endless landscape of dowdy beige houses and bulky brick apartment buildings. Brooklyn was also flat, at least compared to Manhattan. The buildings seemed to huddle low to the ground, as if depressed, or apprehensive.

When we finally pulled up in front of the address Fran had given, I was totally lost. So lost, in fact, that I hadn't the faintest idea where the nearest subway line was. We'd gone under an elevated line at one point, but that had been blocks ago, and who knew which of the three lines—IRT, IND, or BMT—ran on those tracks, or where I might wind up. Greenpoint, or Flatbush, or—

Faintly panic-stricken at the thought of being stranded in Darkest Brooklyn, I hastily asked the driver to wait.

"Yeah, well, the meter'll be running, lady, y'know."

That was fine with me; Dayborne was paying for this. In fact, Dayborne had a corporate account with this cab company, which is actually a pretty standard practice for high-pressure, high-overtime corporations. When you keep employees working until midnight, you pay for their cab home. At least, heartless corporations with a conscience do.

"I'll be right down," I assured the driver, who simply shrugged and hauled a paperback copy of *I, the Jury* out of the glove compartment. Obviously, he was prepared to wait.

Fran Jenkins lived on the top floor of a small two-family house on a nondescript residential street. The house was, save for the color of its paint, identical to the dozen or so houses lining both sides of the street. Trees also lined the street: large unhealthy-looking maples, their leaves wilting in the heat.

I opened the outside door for Fran and helped her climb the long flight of stairs to her apartment. I would have left then, but she clung to me, and was plainly too upset to leave alone. I remembered what a rock she'd been the day before; the poor thing probably hadn't let herself break down while there was still work to be done.

But now she was grieving, and grief pours out all the more violently when it's been suppressed. As she wept on my shoulder, I throttled the irritated thought that Fran's semi-hysteria was excessive. Davis was only her boss, after all, and a real bastard besides. And I bet *he* wouldn't have wept if *Fran* had been murdered instead . . . Guiltily, I realized that my loathing of emotional dependency was making me hard, uncharitable. Davis, and her relationship to him, had been all Fran had. Where was my compassion? Who was I to judge the depth of Fran's loss, or ration the amount of grief she was entitled to display?

"It's okay," I told her, patting her back, "I'll stay and get you settled down. Do you have some bourbon or something, honey? You need a drink."

"Oh, no; I never drink. I—"

"Then I'll make you some nice tea," I announced firmly, and half-pushed Fran into the nearest chair before searching for the kitchen.

The kitchen wasn't hard to find: Fran's apartment wasn't large and it had a pretty standard layout. Front room (parlor), kitchen, bathroom, back room (bedroom). The place was furnished in what might have been the latest retro look but was probably simply Fran's parents' furniture. Overstuffed sofa and chairs, matching end tables and coffee table in the front room; a totally matched bedroom set of high and low dressers, two nightstands, and a full bed complete with head- and foot-board in the back room.

Everything was immaculate; every cloth surface was covered with clear plastic. The windows had Venetian blinds and two layers of curtains (machine lace under and flocked velvet over). The blinds and the lace curtains were closed; the flocked velvet was looped and bound to the side of the window with large satin bows.

Did anyone really live in a place like this? Instantly, I knew the answer was "no." No one lived here, in this diorama of a New York apartment, circa 1955. Fran Jenkins lived her life at her desk at Dayborne. Lived it for her boss, who now was dead.

And what was poor Fran going to do now? As far as I could see, the woman didn't even own a goldfish, or a houseplant.

I did what I could; I put on the kettle, boiled a pot of water, and set a cup of herb tea to steeping. When it looked dark enough—or at least as dark as it was going to get—I stirred in a couple of good dollops of honey and took the resulting potion out to the parlor.

"Here, Fran—you just drink this right down, and then

maybe you should lie down and get some rest." I still thought a stiff shot of bourbon would do her more good, but one makes do with the materials available.

To my surprise, the honey-laced herbal mess seemed to perk Fran up. After a few sips, she became downright loquacious, telling me more than I wanted to know—and probably far more than she really wanted to reveal—about her relationship with the late Abercrombie Davis.

Who was (according to Fran) so kind, so good-looking, so generous . . . "—such a wonderful man to work for; always knew *exactly* how he wanted everything done. And that's the way I did it—not like you girls today, thinking they're as good as a man who's an *executive vice president.*"

"Imagine that," I said after a moment, as some comment seemed called for.

"But they'll take anyone today—it's not like it was when I graduated from business school. Why, I could type ninety words a minute, and take Gregg at one hundred fifty!"

"That's amazing," I said; I meant it, too. Sixty words a minute is considered pretty good typing, and most secretaries these days can't take dictation at all. Not that most bosses know how to dictate anything anymore, either, for that matter. The unholy combination of the Dictaphone and the personal computer has rendered those complementary skills nearly obsolete.

"And I *ran* his offices, you know. I did *everything.* These days girls think they're too good to run errands or—or make coffee—Oh, what am I going to do—I've *always* worked for him, you know—he was in *such* demand he could write his own ticket—and he always took me with him. I was the only girl he trusted, he said; the only one who knew how to treat him right—"

The only one, my cynical mind finished silently, *who*

treated him like a cross between Clark Gable and God Almighty, and who didn't mind being treated in return like a cross between a plantation field hand and a cocker spaniel.

I was so angry at what Fran had let him do to her—at what she'd done to herself, that I couldn't help saying, "I see what you mean: 'My secretary; I think I'll keep her'."

"Oh, Cornelia, you do understand. I thought I was the only one—" Here Fran began to cry again, silently and hopelessly.

Feeling oddly guilty, I helped her wash her face and made her lie down on the bed. She was so far gone in misery she didn't even quibble about mussing the bedspread.

"Now you just lie here and rest," I told her. "And if you need anything, you just call me. I'll leave my number by the phone. And I'm in the Manhattan directory." I knew I was starting to go all-over Southern on her, but I felt guilty and uncomfortable and anxious to be out of there, away from Fran's cloying emotions.

To my surprise and delight, the taxi I'd told to wait had actually waited. I practically flung myself into the cab, thanking the driver profusely; he stared at me as if I'd just dropped in from Mars. "Hey, lady, you said wait. It's already forty-one dollars and fifty cents on the meter; I should worry? So where d'ya wanna go now?"

My watch said 1:10 and my stomach said empty. I considered the matter for all of ten seconds. "First and 52nd," I said.

"You mean back in the city, right?" The driver's voice conveyed deep suspicion; would he be forced further into the Outer Boroughs by a crazy Southern lady?

"Back in the city, right." To New Yorkers, "the city"

means Manhattan. All other boroughs are specifically named, when directions are being given. And First and 52nd is the corner of the street where I live. Fran wasn't the only one who needed to go home and rest for a while.

I was feeling a bit fragile myself.

CHAPTER FIVE

WEDNESDAY AFTERNOON

The cabbie, also eager to return to civilization, got us to the corner of First and 52nd at 1:45. Even though Dayborne's tab was running on this one, I gave the driver ten dollars of my own money as a token of my deep appreciation of his efforts. As the cab charged off into traffic, I made a note of the time so I could fill in today's hours accurately on my time sheet tomorrow. Accounting departments hate fifteen-minute increments, but that is their problem; today I had worked for Dayborne from 9:00 a.m. to precisely 1:45 p.m., and Accounting would just have to deal with the fact. I didn't feel in the least guilty, as nobody at Dayborne would miss me this afternoon. And the loss of a few hours' pay seemed worth it to have the rest of the day off.

Then, feeling oddly shaken by the entire day (not to mention the swift return from Darkest Brooklyn; New York cabbies are all unemployed stunt drivers), I started down 52nd Street toward my apartment building.

When I first fled north to live with my sister, I knew nothing about New York except that it was Up North and Heartless. It was only later, when I'd acculturated, that I realized how fortunate Lizard and I had been.

Because the apartment Grandmother Lispenard had left to Lizard, by way of Waldo, was located in a solid eight-story brick building halfway down a quiet little block that started at First Avenue and dead-ended over the FDR Drive. And unlike most of New York, our block forms its own mini-neighborhood and mutual protection society.

Since Lizard and I were born and bred in Charleston, we didn't care about the fact that New Yorkers Didn't Get Involved, and that traditionally you lived for years in an apartment building and didn't even know your next-door neighbor's name, unless you were gauche enough to look at the names on the mailboxes in the foyer. So of course we talked to everyone: the people peering out of the next-door apartment to see what we were bringing in; the people who ran the fruit store on the corner; the nice older couple who owned the little Hungarian restaurant halfway down the block.

And you know what? The people we talked to liked it, and pretty soon we knew more about that block than people who'd lived there for years. Well, of course we did, honey— it was our home now; you like to know about your home turf, and your neighbors.

What had surprised people at first was discovering we thought of them as neighbors. But despite New York's well-deserved reputation for cold disinterest, no one really likes to be just another face in the cool city crowd. People like to be special. And if there's one thing a Southern girl is good at, it's making people feel special. It's our gift. (Well, it's more Lizard's than mine, in our family—but some of it rubs off on me. Although I did discover that a woman considered icily stand-offish in Charleston was regarded as delightfully warm and charming in Manhattan. Which gave me a rather poor idea of the powers of perception in both cities, but there you are.)

We'd lived on our new block for about six months when someone was mugged right outside our apartment building.

A not-unusual occurrence in New York, any more than it was unusual to have unfamiliar men loitering around—selling drugs, or just waiting for trouble to happen. But this time Lizard happened to be coming home bearing some new canvasboard and a large pizza (with everything, including those disgusting anchovies), and saw what was going on (skinny lout carrying knife trying to rob terrified yuppie carrying briefcase). It wasn't even dark yet. There were some other people around, but nobody was paying any attention; New Yorkers train themselves to not notice things that don't affect them personally.

Lizard, of course, did what any good Southern girl would do in a case like this: started screaming lustily for male assistance (Lizard was the Choral Society's second soprano; she makes a lot of noise for such a little thing). And, just in case the requested male assistance was not forthcoming, she threw the canvasboard, the pizza box, and her box of new pastel crayons at the attacker.

Even in New York, this display attracted attention. And since everyone likes Lizard, she also attracted half-a-dozen assistants, including the owner of the antiques store next door and the two lawyers who lived in the narrow brownstone across the street.

By the time the whole thing was sorted out (the would-be-mugger fled in the confusion; deafened, I hope), and Lizard had explained that no, it was this nice gentleman here who'd been assaulted, one thing was perfectly clear, and it made Lizard livid.

"Why, Neely, *everyone* said they'd thought that man looked suspicious, but not one of them even asked him what he was doing here—on *our* street!"

I pointed out that it was a public street and that Lizard could have gotten hurt. Lizard retorted that she hadn't, and now I saw what came of minding what was supposed to be your own business.

One of the reasons I'd moved North was so that everyone wouldn't know my business—or at least, not *all* of it. But now I had to admit that Lizard had a pretty good point.

Which is how the Far East Fifty-second Street Block Association was really started; no one could stand trying to explain to an indignant Lizard that what went on in the public street in New York City was none of anybody's business.

Oh, don't get me wrong—our Block Association isn't anything formal, or structured. We don't have monthly meetings, or officers, or any silly signs saying, "Citizen Patrol" or "Drug-Free Zone." But after what everyone always refers to as "the day that nice little blonde girl was attacked," things changed a bit.

The big block party a dozen of us (including Lizard and me, and some truly fed-up store owners and some fragile but pugnacious old ladies) browbeat everyone into throwing helped. The party was splashy and fun, and it was the first time some of the people on that street had ever met their neighbors. And everyone got a free "Take Back Our Block" t-shirt, which didn't solve anything, but was a nice gesture on the part of the Merchants' Association that donated them.

The important thing is that we all met, and agreed that we were neighbors. And that neighbors stick together. Or else the neighborhood hangs separately, as Mr. Roscovitz, owner of the Hungarian restaurant, said in his rousing inspirational speech. It was a statement that made a lasting impression on everyone, especially coming as it did as a sort of topper to the mint julep punch Lizard and I had contributed and ladled out with lavish hands. (An old family recipe, of course, and it is inadvisable to set the punch bowl in the vicinity of an open flame.)

So now the block hangs together, after a disorganized fashion.

That isn't to say everyone on the block was a dear true friend, or even generally liked. It does mean that, in the good old-fashioned way, we all have a pretty good idea of who belongs there, and who doesn't. And there are several darling old ladies who now sit openly at their windows scanning the street like advance scouts for Colonel John Singleton Mosby instead of peeking cannily from behind their curtains. And they've got 911 loaded on their quick-dial.

Of course, it's true that people have a right to loiter where they like on a public street.

But it's odd how few of them choose to loiter in front of our building when Dorian-from-down-the-hall is also loitering there with his matched red Dobermans, Bismarck and Rommel; they're sweet little old things, those dogs, they truly are.

After unfolding myself out of the cab, I stopped in the Korean grocery on the south corner and bought myself a pint of Honey Vanilla Häagen-Dazs and some fresh raspberries to soothe my shattered nerves. The nice Korean lady and I agreed it was truly dreadful what fruit prices were coming to, and I added a slice of Well Bred Loaf pound cake to my impulse purchases.

Then I walked on down the block towards our apartment building. As I said, it's a nice little neighborhood: a human-scaled street hemmed in both north and south by the towering impersonal mass of modern skyscrapers. On the corner opposite the Korean fruit store is a fine example of early-1950s modern: a sleek square ten-story apartment house whose white tile brick is usually dingy, like dirty snow. Stores occupy the first floor of this building, including a very convenient pharmacy.

Most of 52nd Street itself is lined in three- and four-story brownstones; some of them are still single occupancy houses, others are now divided into apartments. At ground and sub-ground level some of the brownstones now accommodate stores.

Walking quickly to avoid deadly ice-cream melt, I went past Friendly Footwear Repair (self-explanatory), Butcher-Baker (expensive and utterly delicious meat pies), and The Soap Garden (elegant organic toiletries). Janet, the owner, was reorganizing the window display; she ducked out to say hi. We agreed I was home early, and she said the weather forecast said maybe thunderstorms.

"Great," I said, "maybe it'll cool us off a bit. I've got to go; perishables."

Since the ice cream was probably melting rapidly, I didn't stop to admire the window at Mirror, Mirror (New Age books and related *chatchkes* like magic quartz wands and crystal balls) when I crossed the street. I just waved at Rue, who, like Janet, was occupying a slow buying day by changing the window dressing. Since Rue was trying to get a swathe of silver-star-flocked purple velvet to drape properly, she just looked up and nodded. I made a note to bring Heather by to see the pretty new window when I picked her up later this afternoon.

Just past Mirror, Mirror are three very narrow houses that were probably built around 1850. The first was remodeled sometime in the 1960s and painted extremely bright turquoise; the windows are large circles of bowed glass that make the building look like a popeyed goldfish. I must say it's an interesting landmark.

The second house is a very traditional chocolate brownstone that always seems to be shrinking away from the Mod

Monstrosity beside it. The third, which is brick and which boasts four floors to the others' three, is the narrowest of all. It's almost completely covered with shiny ivy, and houses a literary agency, which is convenient for at least one of the residents of our building.

That brings you almost to the end of the street, and to our own apartment building. Like Grandmother Lispenard, it's a Grand Old Girl: eight stories of foursquare respectability. Built in the days of cheaper land, the building is a rather sprawling squared-off U-shape. On each floor but the eighth, there are four apartments; two in each arm of the U. The connecting bar of the U is the location of the two sets of marble stairs, one flight to each side. There is also a rather uncooperative elevator that's almost as large as the average studio apartment in a modern building.

Because of the building's shape, the main door is reached via a long center courtyard. Halfway between the street and the doorway there's a fountain (which even works, trickling water over the three worn marble bowls in a miserly fashion). A tangle of decorative evergreen bushes hides the basement foundation.

This layout also gives anyone in the sixteen apartments opening on the center court a great view of anyone coming up to the building's front door.

Today Mrs. Goldstein (Apartment 2-C) was sitting looking out her open parlor window. Mrs. Goldstein is a nice Jewish widow with grown children who are always on at her about moving to what they call an "adult home." Mrs. Goldstein, having more sense than her daughter-the-doctor and her-son-the-certified-public-accountant put together, is staying put in the home she's lived in since 1945.

"You're home early today," she called down. "Retired again?"

When I don't feel like working, I don't have to (up to a certain point, of course). So when I need some time off, I simply don't take any assignments for a while. I explain this as "taking my retirement in installments," like Travis McGee.

"Just for the afternoon. How's the afghan coming along?"

"Almost done with this one." Mrs. Goldstein held up an armful of yellow and brown squares. This crochet project was, I knew, slated for the dorm room of Mrs. Goldstein's grandniece, who was starting college at Vassar in the fall. "I could do you one next, if you'd like. I've found a nice pattern all over sprigs of heather—"

"Oh, that would be just lovely!" Like most mothers, I can't resist thematic decorating for my daughter. "That's so sweet of you, Mrs. Goldstein. Look, I've got to get this food inside—why don't I come over later? Then I can pick up anything you want when I go out and get Heather, okay?"

She nodded and withdrew to continue her work; I walked hurriedly past the faintly damp fountain and got to the vestibule without any more interruptions. I buzzed our apartment, but there was no answering buzz to open the door. I hauled my keys out of my handbag and let myself into the lobby. Deciding against the elevator—being stuck between floors with a pint of Häagen-Dazs and no spoon would probably make me lose my temper (which I do have, no matter how much my relatives used to call me "the calm, sensible one"). So I took the stairs, which are better for you anyway.

As I got to the door of our apartment (6-A, which meant our windows looked over the roofs of the little houses next door to the west) I could hear the telephone ringing. Using iron discipline, I did *not* frantically rush to get inside in time to answer it. In the first place, that never works; you always wind up flinging yourself at the phone just as it rings its last before giving up in despair. In the second place, we've got an answering machine, a piece of technology I don't much trust, but which (usually) results in messages.

So I opened the door and entered in a calm, composed fashion suitable to a reasonable adult. "Hey," I called, in case Lizard was actually at home and simply too engrossed in some artistic endeavor to notice reality, "anyone here?" There was no answer, so I assumed Lizard was, indeed, out. Waldo was sleeping in the geometric center of the hallway; at the sound of my footsteps he roused himself to slash perfunctorily at my ankle as I walked by.

When I eventually got to the telephone, after putting the ice cream in the icebox and rinsing the berries and setting them to drain, the little red light on the answering machine was blinking. But when I pushed the "play" button, all I heard was the faint whispery sound of an open line. Then there was a clink and a buzz as whoever it was hung up.

I *hate* it when people do that. In fact, I don't like answering machines at all; I think they're sort of rude. And if you're not even going to leave a message, why not just send a note instead of calling and hanging up?

"Well, shit," I said—which would probably have surprised all those people who think I'm so nice and sweet just because I've got some Charleston drawl left in my voice. But let me tell you, I know all the words, and how to use them, too. I just don't, usually, because I want Heather to be able to use words of more than four letters when she grows up.

However, after that irritating opener, the afternoon improved. I went and changed out of my Perfect Secretary suit (I have five, one for each day of the week) into a pair of jeans that had lasted better than my marriage and a white cotton camisole trimmed with baby blue ribbons that had been part of my trousseau. I still can't imagine what century some of my relatives thought I was marrying into.

Sighing with relief, I washed off my makeup (foundation, blusher, eyeshadow, liner, mascara, lipstick—which takes me precisely ten minutes every morning to apply, and I don't want to *hear* about Letting My Natural Beauty Shine Through, because it won't). I stared at myself critically in the mirror. Pale eyes, pale lashes, pale skin; I looked like a demented white rabbit. I wriggled my nose at myself and unpinned my French twist, shaking my hair loose. My hair, liberated, promptly frizzed around my face in a mass of sandy-reddish exuberance.

Then I padded barefoot to the kitchen and got the ice cream carton out of the icebox and a spoon out of the silverware drawer. And I sat myself down and slowly and deliberately began to eat the Häagen-Dazs Honey Vanilla right out of the little round carton. My enjoyment was enhanced by a vivid mental picture of my mother-in-law's reaction to my treating a Francis I sterling silver teaspoon in this outrageously casual fashion.

Which would serve her right, because my sterling was her fault.

You see, I hadn't wanted Francis I. I thought it was too heavy and ornate: too fussy. I'd wanted Repoussé, which is elegant, feminine, and old-fashioned, its design unchanged from the year it was created, 1828. Repoussé was the pattern I'd registered. Ravenal's mother thought Repoussé wasn't lavish enough for Her Son's Home. So she'd gone around and cancelled my Repoussé listings and reregistered me for Francis I.

I was livid when I found out, but by then it was too late.

And I started married life with a more than complete service of Francis I, including every arcane piece of specialty silverware known to Southern womankind.

Which is why I particularly enjoyed using my sterling as lowly everyday flatware. A small revenge, but mine own.

Upon hearing Noises Kitchen, Waldo condescended to arise and waddle into the room. He sat and glared at me meaningfully.

"Move along, cat," I told him. "You know what the vet said." Which was that Waldo was grossly obese and needed to lose at least five pounds—twenty-five percent of Waldo's body weight, and the equivalent of at least fifty pounds for a human being. Which for some reason unknown to medical science Waldo was not doing, although we dutifully fed him only Hills Feline R/D (light cuisine for cats), which Waldo absolutely refused to eat. I don't know what the damn cat was subsisting on, unless he'd learned to phone for Chicken Delight.

Denied his rights—it was a good thing Waldo couldn't phone a lawyer—he rose and stalked back out of the kitchen.

"If you'd learn to purr, you'd do better," I told his retreating form. My advice was, as usual, ignored; a moment later I heard a metallic thump that indicated Waldo had taken his displeasure with the universe out on The Service. Carrying my ice cream, I went after him and picked the sugar bowl off the floor. Waldo, the obese and lethargic, was nowhere in sight.

"I know who did this," I announced to the apparently empty living room, "and guess what? I don't give a damn. I'll just tell all our guests it got these dents when we hid it from the Yankees."

I thought I heard a faint growl from behind the sofa, but

prudently decided not to press my luck. Instead, I went and tucked up on the padded window seat in the corner of the living room. There I ate ice cream and looked out over the city, and thought about poor Fran and her lonely apartment, and how much luckier I was than she.

After all, when the man in *my* life had died, *my* overwhelming emotion had been relief—

Come to think of it, maybe Fran was luckier after all. If she knew, *she* might feel sorry for *me*. Which was an odd and peculiarly unpleasant thought, so I didn't examine it too hard.

Instead, I started wondering about the murder. As you may have guessed, I'm a mystery reader by obsession; now that I was home and comfortable, I couldn't imagine how I could just have sat there while an entire real murder flowed by me and I didn't ask even one pertinent question.

Such as: "What killed him?"

Which at least was a less upsetting question than, "How could we all have sat there outside his office all day while he was dead inside it?"

Or had it been all day? Perhaps he'd been poisoned at lunch, or at a meeting. No, that wouldn't fit either—he hadn't gone out at all.

When I'd touched his hand, he'd been cold. How long until a once-living body cooled down to room temperature?

This was not a good line of thought; I rose abruptly from the window seat and took the half-empty carton of Häagen-Dazs back to the kitchen. There I re-covered it and shoved it back into the icebox. Then I ran hot water over my hands until they were red and flinched from the water's touch.

The doorbell rang while I was rubbing my hands dry— the apartment door, not the buzzer for the downstairs lobby. Probably Lizard, her arms full of parcels. I padded back down the long hallway and unlocked the door.

"I'm so glad you're here, because I've had the damnedest day," I began, and had the door all the way open before I realized that it wasn't my sister Lizard.

It was Lieutenant Victor Kosciusko.

I'm afraid my first reaction was totally irrelevant relief that at least I wasn't still carrying a half-eaten carton of high-fat ice cream. My second was to wonder what he was doing here.

"I'm sorry about your day," Lieutenant Kosciusko said, continuing to stand there. He was as tall and broad as I'd remembered him; his size somehow reassuring rather than threatening. If he was surprised at seeing Mrs. Upshaw, Perfect Secretary, barefoot in jeans and flimsy camisole with her hair frizzing around her face, he didn't show it. Maybe he was used to seeing people without their daytime disguises. Or maybe he just didn't care what I looked like.

Which was a surprisingly depressing thought, but probably the truth.

"By the way, you should never open your door until you're sure who it is," he went on in a faintly reproving tone.

"I thought it was my sister," I explained. "Because it was the doorbell, not the downstairs buzzer. By the way," I said, echoing him, "how did you get up here?"

"Someone coming in let me in with him. But he made me show my badge first. More people ought to." His tone said that people, in general, didn't; that people, in general, were far too trusting.

I smiled. "We're careful on this block. You were under observation by our spies, too."

"The little old lady watching out the front window?"

Now he smiled too. "That's true—properly nosey neighbors are almost as good as a security patrol."

Suddenly I realized I was keeping him standing on the doorstep. "Oh—would you like to come in?"

"Do you want to see my badge first?"

I shook my head, and he came in and waited while I relocked the door. With a policeman watching, I made very sure I both turned the lock and shot the deadbolt. Since Lizard might be back at any moment, I drew the line at putting the chain-lock on too.

Then I asked if he'd like some coffee. "Or iced tea?" I didn't offer him a mint julep because I was pretty sure policemen on duty didn't drink.

"Thank you, Mrs. Upshaw. Whichever's easier." He followed me down the hallway and stood in the kitchen doorway, watching me haul out glasses and ice and a pitcher of cold tea. "By the way," he said, "aren't you going to ask why I'm here?"

"Well, I just guess I thought you wanted to ask me some more questions, Lieutenant. Oh—this already has sugar in it. Is that okay?"

"Fine," he said, looking rather longingly at the tall glass I was filling with ice cubes. "Yes, I'm afraid I did. Just a few things that came up."

I poured cold tea over the ice cubes and apologized for being out of mint. "Well, we can sit in the front room, and you can ask me anything you like." Terrific; now I was going all-over girlish on him. And an inner voice that sounded suspiciously like my mother was telling me to just run along to the bathroom and quick put on a little lipstick and maybe comb my hair so I didn't look like a fox dragged backwards through a blackberry bush. Oh, and put on some shoes, and a little powder over all those freckles . . .

Shut up, I told the inner voice firmly. Lieutenant Victor Kosciusko was here on business. To help squelch the mental Advice to the Lovelorn column, I touched my wedding ring; a bad luck charm to bring me to my New York senses.

"I don't know what I can tell you," I said, leading the way to the living room, "but I'll be glad to try. Just sit anywhere—" I stopped, because the lieutenant had paused on the threshold and was staring at the main decorative accent in our living room.

"I see you've noticed the Service." I shoved over two creamers and a spoon-rest and set the glasses of iced tea on the space created on the tray. The scrolled silver tray the Service rests upon is approximately a yard wide, and at least keeps wooden tabletops safe from water-rings.

"I'm a trained professional, ma'am; it's my job to notice things." This was said in a flat *Dragnet*-drawl, complete with Joe Friday deadpan expression; then he smiled at me and said, "Sorry. I know you've had a nasty shock and probably want to rest, but—"

"Not as nasty a shock as Mr. Davis had. I hardly knew the man." And hadn't liked what little I'd known. "The one to feel sorry for is Fran."

"That's Frances Jenkins? His secretary?"

"His *executive* secretary. Yes; she's been with him for years and thinks—thought—the damn man walked on water. In the summertime. During a heat wave." Picking up one of the glasses, I curled myself on the sofa, tucking one bare foot under me. "Just sit anywhere—*not there!*"

Lieutenant Kosciusko froze in the act of lowering himself into the big leather armchair across from the couch; without a pause he lithely straightened and turned to look down. Waldo, who'd been doing his justly famed imitation of an overstuffed throw pillow, lifted his serpentine Siamese head and regarded the lieutenant balefully.

"Sorry, boy—is it boy?" Lieutenant Kosciusko, trained professional, asked, unwarily looking to me for confirmation while extending a hand, fingers out, towards Waldo. A friendly gesture, indicating that the man was familiar with cats; unfortunately, he was not familiar with Waldo.

I was, so I yelled, "Waldo, *no!*" and grabbed a small round throw pillow (needlepointed in purple roses by a well-meaning but flora-impaired aunt). To show that when I yelled "no" I meant it, I raised the pillow threateningly. Waldo regarded me balefully, but for once took a gentle hint and hauled himself off the chair.

"I gather," said Victor Kosciusko, who had (trained professional that he was) swiftly and prudently withdrawn his hand, "that he doesn't like policemen."

"That's Waldo. He's not very friendly," I explained, as Waldo stalked off, stomping his paws and muttering Siamese curses under his breath. "Our grandmother left him to us, so we're stuck with him. Our New York grandmother, I mean—our *Charleston* grandmother left us the Service." I indicated the awesome array of sterling monstrosities on the coffee table.

"A family feud?" Lieutenant Kosciusko asked, eyeing the Service doubtfully. It was an understandable assumption.

"Actually, there was a great deal of competition for the Service, believe it or not. And Waldo's not really that bad—he's just old, and cranky, and I guess he misses Grandma Lispenard. She let him get away with murder—"

I stopped, reminded that this wasn't a social call. I guess it reminded Lieutenant Kosciusko, too, because he sat down in the now-vacant leather chair and picked up his iced tea. He drank about half of it before asking his first question.

"You're a mystery fan, Mrs. Upshaw?"

This wasn't exactly a wild guess on his part. Two of the front room walls are covered by bookcases loaded with dead giveaways. I like to collect matched editions of my favorite series, and keep them in alphabetical order, so my interest in Aristocratic Amateur Detectives, Robin Hoods of Modern Crime, and Spunky Female Sleuths was pretty obvious.

"I'm afraid so." With a wall of Lockridge, Grafton, Charteris, and Sayers staring us in the face, I could hardly deny it. "But I promise I don't think I can play detective and solve a real murder. I honestly don't. And I guess you probably think book mysteries are pretty silly."

He smiled at me over the iced tea glass. "Actually, no. I like them. In a murder mystery you have a selection of suspects, an interesting motive, and in the end justice is neatly served. It makes a nice change from real life, where there's usually too much murder and not enough mystery. And the motive's usually pretty simple."

"Oh?"

"Generally it's money. Or else it's what they used to call a crime of passion and now call temporary insanity." He stared down into the dark brown depths of the iced tea. "It's not much like *Murder She Wrote*." Then he looked up again, and this time he wasn't smiling. "Which is why the sudden demise of your Mr. Davis is so unexpectedly interesting."

"It is?" I tried to think what might make this murder particularly interesting to a homicide detective who'd probably seen a lot of them. I couldn't, but a point that had been nagging at me demanded expression.

"Can you tell me what killed him? I've been thinking it was poison, since I heard he was murdered and didn't die of a heart attack like I thought, but—" There didn't seem to be a really good way to end this, so I just stopped babbling.

"What makes you say poison, Mrs. Upshaw? He could have been shot, or stabbed, after all." Lieutenant Kosciusko sounded perfectly casual, but something made me suspect he was taking a deep professional interest in my answer.

"Well, it had to have happened there—at least, I guess it did. So it had to have happened when people were around—you know, Fran and I were at our desks most of the time, and other people were passing by." I remembered the body slumped over the broad expanse of rosewood desk. "I didn't see any blood. And we didn't—I didn't hear a thing—and when I touched him, he was cold—"

Cool to the touch, because he'd been lying there for hours; maybe all day. Maybe if we'd noticed earlier, the paramedics could have saved him—

"Mrs. Upshaw?" Lieutenant Kosciusko's voice was gentle, but firm. "There wasn't anything you could have done for him."

I regarded him doubtfully; this sounded like mendacious professional comfort for the hysterical civilian. He shook his head.

"No, I mean it. By the time you found him, nothing would have helped. Because he'd been dead for at least two days."

I'm afraid I stared at him with my mouth hanging half-open for about ten seconds. Then I said, "You mean he was dead all the time? Before we even got there? All *day?*" My voice sounded oddly high, faintly hysterical.

"That's right. So we have a traditional locked room mystery—or would have, if he hadn't been poisoned. Poison makes it easier. For the murderer, anyway."

"So I was right."

"Yes, Mrs. Upshaw. Do you know what the poison was?"

"Am I a suspect?" This sounded almost hopefully suspicious, even to me. I guess I was more rattled by the whole mess than I'd thought. My next thought was that if Dayborne didn't have such ferociously efficient air-conditioning, it would have been pretty obvious that Davis hadn't been newly dead—

"I'm afraid not," he told me soothingly. "Well—not a very serious one, anyway. It was cyanide in his coffee. Actually, whoever did it is just lucky he's not going to be up on multiple homicide charges. Or she, of course. Anyone could have walked in and been offered a cup."

"No," I said slowly, "because Mr. Davis was a—" I stopped, feeling that odd reluctance to tell the truth about the newly dead that most of us suffer from.

"We've already gathered he wasn't exactly a little friend to all the world," the lieutenant said. "Consider the description understood. Why couldn't anyone have drunk it?"

"Because Davis only drank this special expensive blend that he bought himself; something imported. His coffee wasn't made in the staff kitchen, either; Fran kept his stash under lock and key and brewed him up two fresh pots a day. First thing in the morning and then again after lunch. He didn't like stale coffee, either. And he never offered it to anyone else."

"If someone went in and poured himself a cup? Without asking?"

I shook my head. "Not the way it is done around Dayborne. They pride themselves on a very structured corporate culture. Coffee there isn't taken, it's offered. From the upper ranks to the lower, too, and never the other way around. Like—like a gracious gesture from the lord to the serf. Besides, Davis had a rotten temper and a petty mind and nobody wanted to get on his bad side."

Lieutenant Kosciusko frowned slightly and rattled ice cubes around his glass. "Let me get this straight—let's say I were a vice president at Dayborne. I couldn't offer the president a cup of coffee?"

I laughed. "Lieutenant, they don't have 'vice presidents' at Dayborne. They have junior vice presidents, administrative vice presidents, assistant vice presidents, associate vice presidents, and senior vice presidents. Oh, and executive vice presidents, which outrank all the others. I don't think they've even *got* a president. They've got corporate vice presidents, too, but that's more of an honorary title for retirees than anything else."

"Oh," said the lieutenant, rather meekly, and stared intently at his half-melted ice cubes. There was a brief hiatus in the official proceedings as I offered more iced tea and went off to refill our glasses.

When I came back, Lieutenant Kosciusko was standing in front of one of Lizard's paintings: adorable elf-child and equally adorable winged cat. "That's my sister's," I said, handing him his glass. "She's a book cover artist. That was the cover painting for *The Glass Princess*. The elf is my daughter, Heather."

He admired the painting, and the elf. "Is that a good likeness?"

"Good enough, except for the wings." Unable to help myself (doting mothers have no self-control), I picked up a silver-framed photograph to show him. "This is Heather."

He looked at the picture, and then at me; I didn't wait for the comment I was sure he was going to make, because people always do. "She takes after her father's side of our family," I said, and set the picture back on the bookcase shelf. I already know Heather doesn't look much like me. "Now, what about this murder?"

A bit abrupt, but murder was what Lieutenant Kosciusko had come to see me about, after all. He picked up his cue promptly and gracefully.

"I don't suppose," he said, "someone might have poisoned Davis because they weren't offered coffee? Or were, if they outranked him? Dayborne-ly speaking, of course."

"Well, he was an executive vice president. That's the highest adjective they've got. So he had to offer everyone else coffee—but he didn't."

If all this about coffee etiquette sounds awfully petty, that's because it is. But pettiness is one of the hallmarks of corporate life, which is one of the many very good reasons I prefer temp work.

"I see," said the lieutenant. "Of course, we're not sure the cyanide was in the pot—it could have been dropped into the cup he was drinking at the time."

"But can't you tell? I mean, the forensic tests—" Then I suddenly realized where this was leading and I stopped talking abruptly. "Oh," I said.

"That's all right—Ms. Jenkins has already told us she threw out the old coffee and washed the cup and the pot. Unfortunate, but not unusual?" This last was a question; I felt him watching me, ready to gauge my response.

"No, it wasn't in the least unusual." Not for Fran, the over-eager office helpmate. "Fran's a very—tidy sort of person. She never leaves anything lying around; she's always tidying up after her boss. He couldn't stand a mess; I saw him sweep everything off a junior VP's desk onto the floor one day just because the desk was piled with papers and it annoyed him."

"I see," said Lieutenant Kosciusko. "A man of strong opinions, was he?"

"Very. And there wasn't any reason not to clean up. I mean, we didn't think there was anything wrong—well, except that he was dead, of course, but I never thought of murder—"

"Not even after that anonymous letter?"

I shook my head. "Fran said he got a lot of those; she has a whole file of them. She said he—they didn't take them seriously."

"I see," he said. After a moment, he asked, "You said you didn't see Mrs. Davis on Friday afternoon. But that she called up from the lobby?"

"That's right." I felt oddly uneasy; I thought I knew where this was heading.

"Did you see her at all after that? Oh, say, when you were leaving at five? Was she waiting downstairs in the main lobby?"

I found myself assessing my answer, taking time to choose my words. For words I spoke now, to this homicide detective, would possess a weight that might bring the Law's hand to heavy rest. I didn't want to get anyone into trouble they didn't deserve.

But a man had been murdered. He hadn't been a very nice man, but that's not a capital offense. And there were people who missed him, and grieved. For all I knew, his widow was as prostrate with grief as poor Fran. Mind, I doubted it. But it was possible . . . .

"I didn't see her there," I said.

"Or in a car or a cab? Waiting at the curb, say?"

Dutifully, I tried to think back to Friday afternoon, when I'd been dashing off, happily planning the weekend ahead. Frankly, I hadn't noticed much of anything but myself. I shook my head. "No. I didn't see her."

"I see. And you were at your desk all day?" This seemed to be backtracking, but doubtless Lieutenant Kosciusko had his reasons.

Yes, I'd been at my desk steadily, except for a few breaks; I told him the times. "Of course," I added, "anyone could have come by after I left at five. Or he could have gone in Saturday, and—"

Lieutenant Kosciusko was shaking his head. "I'm afraid not, Mrs. Upshaw. His wife says he never came home Friday night. In fact, she says she hadn't seen him since he left for work Friday morning."

"Well for heaven's sake, didn't she even wonder where he was?"

"Apparently," said the lieutenant, "they aren't close. She says it wasn't unusual." There was no inflection whatsoever in his voice.

"There are marriages like that." I tried to make my voice just as noncommittal; just as expressionless. I don't think I entirely succeeded. Suddenly I was tired, and utterly depressed. "Look, Lieutenant, I didn't poison Mr. Davis and I don't know who did. And I have to go pick up my daughter—"

"Of course. I'm sorry to have to put you through this, Mrs. Upshaw. If you—"

"—think of anything, or the murderer suddenly confesses, I promise I'll call you." I smiled, to show him I knew that last bit was just a joke.

"Well, then." He paused, looked around, and finally set his empty glass gingerly beside the Service's sugar tongs. "Thank you for the iced tea. I suppose—" Whatever he'd been going to say, he didn't.

And that was about that, except that as I was watching

Lieutenant Kosciusko start down the stairs, Lizard came dashing up, pausing for the briefest of moments to assess him with professional sisterly interest. "Wow," she said, darting up to kiss my cheek, "is that a Gentleman Caller at last? I'll have to call Mom and Aunt Lady and Cousin Vangie right away. They'll be ecstatic."

"Oh, shut up," I said with sisterly affection. "He's not a Gentleman Caller; he's a homicide detective. He just came to ask me a few more questions, that's all."

"Sure he did," said Lizard. She dropped her assorted parcels in the middle of the hall and dug a small box out of her huge shoulder bag. "I know! Look, I just got a new deck at Rue's. Just close your eyes and pick a card, any card."

By which she meant yet another new tarot deck; I don't know why she collects them, as she can't shuffle cards worth a damn and is always complaining about the artwork. Still, Lizard is ever the optimist.

To save time and avoid trouble in the home, I obligingly closed my eyes and pulled one card out of the middle of the fanned deck Lizard was holding out. "It's the ace of spades, right?" I opened my eyes and turned the card over. A man and a woman entwined, naked, in front of an apple tree. A serpent coiled about the trunk of the apple tree. The man and woman looked fatuous. The serpent looked smug.

"Ha!" said Lizard in triumph, peering at The Lovers. You didn't have to be Sherlock Holmes to figure out what *that* card meant.

"I'm going to pick up Heather," I told Lizard in disgust. "There's some ice cream in the icebox and berries in the drainer. See you later." I snatched my keys from the hook beside the door.

"Neely, honey," said my baby sister sweetly, "don't you

think you ought to put your shoes on first? Oh, and give me back my card, okay?"

There are times, rare but heartfelt, when I think my sister Lizard gets way too much fun out of life.

Real life being what it is (plotless and anticlimactic), I put on my walking shoes and changed my Victorian camisole for a shirt before braving the city streets. Then I settled into stride for the walk down to Metropolitan Office Professionals.

I like walking; one of the reasons I love New York is because you can walk almost endlessly, through dozens of mini-worlds. Chinatown, Little Italy, the Village, the Wall Street jungle. Uptown, along Madison and Fifth, where the window-shopping alone is worth the effort. And it's good exercise for body and brain; I seem to stretch my mind along with my legs. Maybe it's the extra oxygen hitting the little gray cells. Anyway, it's a good time to think.

And today I certainly had a lot to think about.

So J. Abercrombie Davis (I never did find out what the "J" had stood for) had been murdered. Poisoned. Cyanide in his coffee. And he'd been killed—when?

Sometime after five on Friday, when I'd hustled Fran out of there so fast to avoid one of his last-minute fake-outs: "Oh, Fran, before you go would you just fax this memo to our Bangladesh office?" And it would be ten pages, and as far as I know, the Bangladesh office has never picked up its phone or fax in living memory.

And Fran would, just because Davis had asked her to.

Davis had most certainly been alive at 3:30 that Friday afternoon, when he'd been explaining to an unfortunate junior vice president that his preliminary quarterly report was substandard. Explaining at top volume, with his office door open. When the poor little JVP had slunk out clutching his folders, I'd stared hard at the letter I was writing to my brother, pretending I—and the rest of the corridor—hadn't heard a thing.

Just after that, Davis had stalked down the hall. When he'd returned at 4:00, he'd paused to snap out an order that Fran was to hold all his calls. He'd then slammed his office door, and that was the last time I'd seen the ever-amiable J. Abercrombie Davis alive.

And I'd left Dayborne promptly at 5:00 p.m. that Friday.

So that left Friday night, Saturday, and maybe Sunday. Probably Friday night; Davis hadn't gone home, or called.

Correction: His wife *said* he hadn't. (No detail slips past us Spunky Female Sleuths.) So . . .

Here my train of thought went on hold as I paused for a red light, then wove across the street between oncoming cars with the other feral New York pedestrians while a couple of obvious out-of-towners hesitated on the corner, waiting timidly for the "walk" light. New York is a professional city; it's no place for amateurs. When I reached the opposite side of the street, I tried to resume my brilliant deductions where I'd left off.

Wife, that was it. Maybe Davis *had* gone home, and—

And been poisoned by his not-so-loving spouse, who had then somehow trucked his body back to Dayborne, carted it up to the twenty-first floor, and arranged it in his office? Well, scratch that scenario.

I tried to remember what I'd learned about cyanide in my years of reading murder mysteries, which turned out to be not much. Cyanide was one of the most deadly of the poisons; it smelled of bitter almonds, and was found in such unlikely places as apricot pits. At least, I thought it was apricots.

But there was one thing I did know for sure about cyanide poisoning.

Death was almost instantaneous.

So, since Davis would have died almost immediately after he ingested the cyanide, it had to have been in his office. Which meant someone had come in and dropped cyanide in his coffee. Into the cup, or into the pot? Either was possible, but my preference was for the cup. More certainty that the victim would drink the deadly dose; less chance that he'd suddenly decide he didn't want any more caffeine that day, and have his secretary toss the pot of waiting coffee.

It wouldn't be difficult to doctor the cup; just wait until Davis was looking away. Or even pour him a fresh cup and drop the poison in then.

So that was how. Which left who. Also why. Method, motive, opportunity. Method was established. Opportunity wouldn't be difficult to arrange. Motive . . .

Money or passion, Lieutenant Kosciusko had said. Who profits? Who hates?

Or who loves? I tried to imagine anyone killing Davis for love rejected; it was, I supposed, possible.

Just as, I realized, it was possible that Brittany Davis hadn't really left at all last Friday. She could have waited until the office support staff had mostly gone home, and then simply waltzed back up to her husband's office to slip a little poison into his coffee cup.

But why should Brittany kill him? For money? Divorce was easy, and any good lawyer could get Brittany Davis quite a nice divorce settlement. Without eliminating Brittany Davis as a suspect, I set her aside for the moment, and went on to consider Davis's business associates.

Who at Dayborne might want Davis dead? Really dead,

not just making an idle wish in the aftermath of a run-in with a man who had apparently thrived on confrontation and conflict. There were a number of possibilities.

Was it someone who wanted Davis's office, or his budget line? Someone Davis was blocking from promotion? Or maybe—

The broad expanse of East 23rd Street loomed before me; one does *not* attempt to bull-dance across the big two-way traffic cross-streets if one has any sense of self-preservation at all. Several people dashed across like demented squirrels, to the *leitmotif* of blaring horns and some imaginative swearing by a Pakistani taxi driver who seemed to be supremely fluent in English slang. I waited for the light.

South of 23rd, I swung west towards Fifth and MOP. It was past 4:00 now, and traffic, both vehicular and pedestrian, was already starting to thicken in preparation for rush hour. Heat rose from the streets and sidewalks in a palpable wave. Tomorrow was supposed to be a scorcher.

The offices of Dayborne Ventures were, of course, thoroughly air-conditioned. Would that have affected the apparent time of death? But I was sure that NYPD's forensics department would have allowed for that—

You will note, by the way, that I was doing precisely what I had sworn to Lieutenant Kosciusko less than two hours ago that I would not do. I noticed this myself, and shut up the faint voice of my not-very-uneasy conscience by telling myself that I was *not* playing detective. I was just wondering, that was all.

After all, I was, however temporarily, employed at Dayborne; naturally I had a mild interest in the matter. Of course, I wasn't going to be employed at Dayborne much longer—maybe for another hour or so, I thought.

I was wrong. When I arrived at MOP, Holly Steinberg
waylaid me and told me Dayborne had called and wanted
me to finish out the rest of my allotted stint as Annabel
Price's replacement.

"Why?" I asked. "The boss is dead."

"Long live the boss, I guess," Holly said, shrugging. "I
mean, Dayborne'll have to put someone in that spot to fill
in, and he—or she," Holly added conscientiously, "will
keep right on needing secretarial backup. Ours not to
reason why; ours but to bill—But if you're not okay with
working there now, I'll get you out of Dayborne today. Just
say the word."

As I've said, Holly's very mother-hennish about her temporary chicks. I smiled and assured her I was just fine there.
And that I'd be just delighted to finish out the Dayborne assignment.

In retrospect, I can see that I should have told Holly yes,
get me out of Dayborne and into a new assignment *right
now*. And the thought even crossed my mind, briefly, at the
time. But it did seem rather like deserting a sinking ship.
Besides, with Davis gone, the worst feature of the Dayborne
job had been eliminated—an unworthy thought, but of
course I thought it anyway. I'm frequently accused of pos-
sessing a nasty mind.

And to be perfectly frank, I wanted to see what would
happen, as I admitted to Brenda Frostheim that evening as
I helped her shuffle manuscripts from the unsteady piles
they were stacked in onto actual storage shelves. It's a big
job; paper weighs a lot more than most people think, especially in 800-page chunks. Remember that I told you the literary agency on our block was convenient for one of our
neighbors? That neighbor is Brenda Frostheim, who occu-

pies one of the two eighth-floor apartments of our Grand Old Girl of a building.

There are only two apartments on that floor. Once the building's owner lived in one apartment and the building's manager lived in the other. As you can imagine, the two top-floor apartments are definitely the high-priced spreads. They're huge, a veritable dream of space and luxury involving working fireplaces, built-in bookcases, teak parquet floors, and servants' quarters.

Brenda owns the east-side-of-the-building apartment. This gives her a smashing view over the East River; it also gives her a rather noisy view over the FDR Drive. Brenda says she finds the traffic noises soothing, which is a good thing.

The apartment itself, as I said, is stone luxury. However, it is furnished in a rather haphazard style I shall, for lack of a better descriptive term, dub "Early Library." Despite the yards of built-in bookcases, books still spill over every even semi-flat surface.

Books on every subject imaginable, too: astronomy, medieval history, needlework, sadomasochism, horse racing, herbs, rocket science, camping—you name it, Brenda owns at least one book on the subject. Brenda's book collection makes mine look modest, which will give you some idea of how many books *she* has.

Any space not occupied by books is piled with magazines—again, on every conceivable and inconceivable subject. Stacks of *History Today* jostle *Car Fancy* for space. *Police Chief* and *Soldier of Fortune* battle *Romantic Times* and *Writer's Digest* for *lebensraum*. And stray issues of *Publisher's Weekly* are encountered everywhere.

From these subtle clues, you've probably deduced that our Brenda is a writer. With a grim dedication that I can only admire and never hope to emulate, Brenda has managed to become a full-time, work-at-home-all-day professional in a field where most practitioners spend their lives as wistful Wannabees.

Brenda was supposed to be a schoolteacher: her parents' idea. Her first book was handwritten on sheets of lined yellow paper while she was still in college. So was her second. She wrote her third while teaching seventh-grade English at the Centerville, Iowa, junior high school.

"Whenever did you find the time?" I asked her once, awed by her achievement.

"You don't *find* time," Brenda told me, "you *make* it."

Brenda Frostheim made her time by getting up at 4:30 in the morning and writing until 6:00; by staying up until midnight; by refusing all social invitations; by writing all day Saturday and Sunday and every holiday. By ruthless dedication.

For her twenty-fifth birthday, Brenda bought herself an electric typewriter. Then she took those three handwritten books and typed them up in proper manuscript format. When they were done, she wrapped them up and mailed them to Stratford Books, the leading publisher of historical romance. Then she sat down and started book number four.

Stratford bought Brenda's books; her editor cautioned Brenda against over-optimism. Most books sink without a trace soon after publication.

Brenda's books didn't. For her twenty-seventh birthday, Brenda bought herself a top-of-the-line word processor and a laser printer. And doubled her output.

For her thirtieth birthday, Brenda quit her school teaching job, moved to New York, and bought herself Apartment 8-East.

You probably know her professional name: Arden Frost. Arden is the best-selling author of *Dazzling Time*, *Timeless Flame*, *Time's Pirate*, and at least two-dozen others. (Frankly, I can't keep their titles straight. Brenda once confided, under the influence of an Upshaw mint julep punch, that she couldn't either.)

I'd promised to give her a hand clearing some space in her office that evening, and since Brenda is a writer, I thought she might have some good ideas on solving the Dayborne murder. But when I explained this to her, Brenda looked at me and said, "But Cornelia, I'm a romance writer, not a detective," in her best (i.e., really lousy) Dr. McCoy Southern drawl. Then, after I explained the case to her, she said, "You know, I think you'd better just get out of there. Poisoners aren't nice people."

Which seemed a bit inadequate, but I just smiled and said, "Well, no one wants to poison me, and I can't just desert Dayborne in its hour of need."

"Sure you can," said Brenda, looking stubborn, which she does very well indeed. Brenda's not what you'd expect a best-selling romance author to look like, if you've never met one before. She's a bit on the plump side; her face is pleasant rather than pretty, remarkable only for a rather firm jaw. Her chief claim to beauty is her hair, which is magnificent: thick and wavy and the color of pouring maple syrup, and long enough for her to sit on. Mostly, however, Brenda just curls this natural wonder up on top of her head and jabs hairpins into the resultant mass until it stays put.

Usually it doesn't stay put very long; Brenda spends a lot of time absently re-stabbing pins into her hair. Which was what she was doing this very minute, even as she scolded me. "You don't give a flying fig about Dayborne, Cornelia—and what makes you think no one wants to poison you? Maybe you were the real target."

"Why?" I asked.

"Because you can type and the other secretaries can't?" Brenda offered, and we both laughed. "Because you know too much," Brenda continued, and that somehow didn't seem as funny. Then Brenda fixed her large maple-syrup-amber eyes on me and said, "You won't leave because you want to see what will happen."

I wanted to deny this—but I had to admit that she was right. "When else will I ever get the chance to see a murder mystery in action?" I tried to keep my tone flippant; I thumped one two-ream-manuscript down on the lowest shelf and added, "Brenda, honey, have you ever considered writing short stories instead?"

"No money in them," Brenda said. "Margo would *kill* me." Margo is Arden Frost's literary agent; Margo's agency occupies the narrow vine-covered brick house down the street. As I said, convenient. "And don't change the subject. Murder's dangerous. Promise you won't try to play Harriet Vane, okay?"

Why does everyone tell me not to meddle in murder? I mean, I *know* Real Life isn't like a murder mystery. "I'm not. Now, where does this stuff go?"

That was how I spent Tuesday evening. You see? No amateur detecting at all. The discussion Brenda and I had over Sedutto's frozen yogurt—which Brenda insists, in the teeth of the information on the label, has fewer calories than ice cream—concerning the psychology of poisoners and the *qui bono* question didn't count, being purely academic, in aid of the creation of a suitable villain for the next Arden Frost opus.

CHAPTER SIX

THURSDAY

"Cornelia, would you please come into my office for a moment when you're free?"

This was a 9:05 interoffice call from Nelson Branagh. Translated from the surface politeness of business speak, it meant, "Please get in here right this minute."

"I'll be right there," I told him. "Mr. Branagh wants to see me," I added to Fran as I hung up.

Believe it or not, when I'd walked in that Wednesday morning at 8:45, Fran was already sitting at her desk. She was typing energetically, red-eyed but determined. As I spoke, she stopped and looked up. "Oh? What about?"

"I haven't the faintest idea," I said, and shut and locked my desk (never walk away without doing that; trust me on this) before heading down to find out what Mr. Branagh wanted with me.

All I knew about Nelson Branagh was that he was a senior vice president; he occupied the rung of the corporate ladder just below Davis's. Branagh had that patented Dayborne Look: sleek, slick, heavily successful. When I walked into his office (window, but not corner), he bent upon me the compassionate look of a worried shark.

"Good morning, Cornelia," he said. "Terrible thing to have happen while you're filling in here. I hope it hasn't put you off Dayborne—we don't usually have this sort of thing happen."

"Oh, not at all, Mr. Branagh. My opinion of Dayborne hasn't changed in the least," I assured him.

"Well, that's good. But I'm not as formal as poor old Davis—call me Nelson."

"Thank you," I said, "but I'd rather not. I think a little formality's good for an office, Mr. Branagh."

"Well, of course, Cornelia—"

"Which is why I prefer to be called Mrs. Upshaw."

This stopped him in his verbal tracks for a moment as he regarded me suspiciously: was I trying to be funny? For a moment he surveyed me from my polished black leather pumps to my disciplined French twist. Apparently I impressed Branagh as being both adult and non-facetious, because he stopped trying to achieve an impossible combination of jovial good humor and solemn respect for the dead and returned to a more normal tone of voice.

"Well, that's fine, Mrs. Upshaw." Now he was brisk, efficient; executive. "Have a seat; there's something I'd like to discuss with you, if I may."

I already had my suspicions as to what he wanted to discuss—and it wasn't what you're probably thinking, either. I was right, too: Nelson Branagh was offering me a position as a permanent member of the Dayborne corporate family.

"I've seen your work, and Davis thinks—thought very highly of you. Everyone does, in fact."

"That's awfully sweet of them," I murmured, regarding my hands modestly.

"And I think you're just what I want on my team." A hint of complacency crept into his voice, and an instant later I knew why. "You see—Mrs. Upshaw—I'm the new Executive Vice President of Corporate Restructuring and Accounts. And I'd like you to be my executive secretary. Would you be interested?"

"Congratulations, Mr. Branagh." Suddenly there were two people inside my brain: Mrs. Upshaw the secretary making the proper responses and Cornelia the Self-styled Sleuth wondering if Nelson Branagh had thought an EVP worth killing for. "But what about Fran Jenkins? I mean, she's been in that position—"

"With Davis," Branagh said. "Frankly—and I don't mean to denigrate her, because I know she works hard and goes that extra mile—but I just don't think she's got the flexibility and talent for modern business. She's a little— old-fashioned."

By which the smug son-of-a-witch meant that Frances Jenkins was middle-aged and plump and didn't look like a slumming runway model. The fact that she was competent and loyal to a fault (witness her devotion to J. Abercrombie Davis) meant nothing.

"So how about it? You don't have to answer right now, but think about it for a few days. If you're interested, we can get together and discuss an employment package. You know, an office professional with your skills doesn't have to waste her time doing temp work."

"Oh, wow, I hadn't any idea!"—I did *not* say. I wanted to, but I controlled myself and promised Branagh that I would, indeed, think about his offer.

"But I'd just hate to think I was stealing someone else's job." My voice was so honey-sweet I nearly gave myself diabetes; I did not quite flutter my eyelashes.

"Trust me, Cornelia—er, Mrs. Upshaw—you won't be." Branagh attempted a look of boyish ruefulness that he was way too old for. In my book, "boyish" doesn't sit well on any male over the age of eighteen. "You've worked with her for a few weeks, now, and I'm sure you'll agree that Fran will be happier elsewhere."

"Too many happy memories in Corporate Restructuring and Accounts," I suggested, and Branagh nodded gravely.

"I'm glad you understand."

"I'm glad I do." I understood all too clearly that with her boss gone, Fran Jenkins would be forced out of her beloved home, Corp. Res. & Accts. Feeling we were pretty well done here, I smiled noncommittally and stood up. Branagh rose when I did and walked me to his office door; two points for him. There he shook my hand and urged me once again to think over Joining Our Corporate Family and I assured him once again that I surely would.

As I walked back towards my desk, I surely did think it over. So now it would be Nelson Branagh, EVP, Corp. Res. & Accts. A major promotion; a raise in pay; a corner office; an executive secretary of his very own, and an assistant secretary for his secretary.

Worth a lot, especially to a man on the corporate fast track rise. Worth fighting for.

Worth killing for?

I'd hoped to be able to sit quietly at my desk and continue this mental philosophical discussion while collating twenty copies of a forty-page report. This was not to be—at least, not at that point—because when I got back to Corp. Res. & Accts., we had a visitor.

The widow. Mrs. J. Abercrombie Davis. The second.

The second Mrs. Davis, that is. Brittany. The trophy model. Which is what they call it these days when a man ditches the wife who helped him become successful in favor of a new model half his age who makes him *look* successful.

As I'd told the detectives yesterday, I'd seen her once before; a week ago she'd come by to meet her husband because they had tickets for a major Broadway musical. That was the evening Davis kept his wife, his executive secretary,

and me there until 7:40 p.m. finishing up a last minute ur-
gent-and-vital report. Which meant Lizard had to pick up
Heather, which meant Lizard and Julian had to change their
plans, and while Lizard swore she and Julian were just as
happy to stay home and watch TV while babysitting
Heather, I was still pretty pissed at Davis. On the other
hand, I get paid for each hour-or-portion-thereof and for
every hour-or-portion-thereof, and MOP double-bills for
time after 5:00 p.m., which was some consolation.

I don't know if Mr. and Mrs. Davis made the opening
curtain, but I do know Mrs. D. was also pretty damned
pissed about it, because we could hear her comments as she
and Davis left while Fran and I finished locking up. She
sounded like one of the less well-bred felines in the Winter
Garden Theater—a cat in a very bad mood indeed.

"I understand her feelings," I'd said. "Look on the
bright side—maybe a chandelier will land on his head."

Fran was Not Amused. "She just doesn't understand
that business has to come first," Fran had told me reprovingly.

Now the supposedly grieving widow was standing in
front of Fran, who was standing in front of the late J. Abercrombie Davis's door. Fran was still dressed in severe and
funereal black. Mrs. Davis wore a vivid turquoise dress in a
much-buttoned pseudo-military style that looked as if she
were trying the garment out for a younger and smaller
sister. In addition to a Gucci handbag, she was, for some
reason, holding a stuffed toy under one arm.

Still mentally playing detective, I wondered why Brittany
Davis was here. I found out in about ten seconds, because
as I walked up she rounded on me—a neat trick on those
spike heels. The mass of her expensively streaked blonde
hair made her look like an angry cat. The stuffed toy ut-

tered a small whuffle of distress; I found myself staring into big round eyes as brown and limpid as my daughter's. Brittany wasn't carrying a stuffed toy, she was carrying a small dog, a brown-and-white spaniel whose long flowing ears were getting tangled in Brittany's gilt buttons.

When I politely mentioned this, Brittany swore and shoved the spaniel at me. "Here, you hold the damn thing, will you?" I found myself with an armful of spaniel; Brittany brushed dog hair from turquoise silk. The spaniel cuddled against me and gazed up with hopeful chocolate eyes.

"The office is no place for animals," Fran said, regarding this exchange with prim disapproval. I was pretty sure she meant the dog.

"Look, can't you talk some sense into Marabel Morgan here?" Brittany demanded of me. "Or better yet, just let me into my husband's office." Brittany eyed Fran balefully; Fran's face was a mask of only semi-repressed distaste.

"I'm sorry, but I can't do that," I said, which didn't go over real big with Brittany.

She turned her brilliant contact-lens-green glare my way, and was plainly about to light into me next; I cut in with, "And neither can Ms. Jenkins. Because as you can see, the police still have it sealed up."

Since the door to her husband's office was still criss-crossed with yellow-and-black tape and had a big sticker smack dab in the middle saying, "Crime Scene Do Not Disturb," I thought this ought to have been pretty obvious. And if Brittany really wanted either Fran or me to break a police seal for her, Brittany ought to learn to be a lot nicer about how she asked us serfs for favors.

"Oh," she said, just as if she hadn't noticed. "Well, actually, all I want is his checkbook. Couldn't you just . . . ?" She let this trail off suggestively.

Fran ignored her utterly, a tactic which forced me into the center court. I set the little spaniel down and held its rhinestone-studded leash out to Brittany, who apparently couldn't see me anymore. I dropped the leash on the floor.

"I'm sorry," I said again. "May I suggest you ask the police for it, Mrs. Davis?" This was just plain mean on my part; Brittany *hated* being called Mrs. Davis. I could see her point, of course.

Apparently Brittany already had, and been refused, because now she shut up and stalked off in a pea-green huff. You just can't flounce in a skirt that short and that tight, you know. A moment later I heard the large glass door to the receptionist's lobby close with a stifled boom that meant someone had done her level best to slam the unslammable.

"I guess Brittany's a little upset," I said to Fran after a moment. "I wonder why she wanted his checkbook, particularly? Doesn't she have her own?"

"She's a *bitch*," Fran practically hissed, and for a moment looked truly vicious. Then she blinked, and her eyes filled with tears, which I pretended not to see. And her comment suddenly reminded me of something.

The dog. When Brittany had attempted to flounce out, she had flounced without her dog. I looked around and spotted the end of the leash; the spaniel had disappeared under my desk. I grabbed the leash and tugged and the dog reappeared.

"I'll be right back," I said, and hurried down the hall toward Reception, the spaniel trotting beside me.

But when I got there, the only person in Reception was Amber, who was re-applying her lipstick. Brittany Davis was already gone. I considered chasing her down to the lobby, but she could be long gone by the time I got there. I

117

looked down at the spaniel and decided the best thing to do was hang onto it until Brittany got over her mad and remembered her dog.

"She'll be back for you," I told the spaniel, who waved her white plume of a tail and happily followed me back to my desk. "Sorry, Fran," I said as I approached, "but Mrs. Davis forgot her dog."

"She would." Fran's voice was coldly bitter. "She hates that dog because *he* gave it to her. She didn't deserve him." Fran grabbed up an already mangled clump of Kleenex and dabbed. "Do you know she wouldn't even tell me where the funeral's going to be held?"

"Someone here will know," I said, interjecting the voice of reason. "Don't cry, honey—she's just all upset and so are you."

This should have been obvious even to the most self-absorbed. Today Fran didn't look middle-aged, but old; the dark dress she was wearing in her self-imposed mourning was too harsh for an aging woman. Her makeup, thickly applied in an attempt to hide the ravages of grief, had become a blotchy mask.

"This has been awful rough on you," I went on soothingly. "Look, I'll get you a glass of water, okay?"

Fran nodded and the spaniel and I beat it along to the water cooler in the staff lunchroom. Just as I was filling Fran's tea mug with ice water, Carolyn Eaton walked in. Carolyn Eaton didn't look old, or tired; in her tasteful blue-gray skirted suit and perfect yet subdued business makeup she looked like precisely what she was: the hopeful young Dayborne executive on the rise.

"Oh, hello, Cornelia." Then, staring down at the dog, "What's that?"

"It's a dog," I said, without amplifying.

"Oh." Carolyn reverted to her previously-scheduled speech. "Cornelia, has Branagh talked to you yet?"

When I allowed as to how he had, Carolyn smiled in a do-let-me-convince-you fashion and said how very glad they'd all be to have me aboard. "You know everyone here thinks very highly of your work. Harriet always said—says that you're worth any two other secretaries she's ever met."

"That's so kind of her," I said, and asked if Carolyn knew how Harriet was doing.

"As well as can be expected," Carolyn said, "and she knows there's a promotion waiting for her, so I'm sure she'll be back in no time." She smiled, doubtless to show that this was what passed, at Dayborne, for humor.

"I'm so glad," I said, and then (oh, so casually) asked if Carolyn would be promoted now too.

"Well . . . something *may* happen. But don't say anything about it yet." This was conveyed to me in a *sotto voce* conspiratorial tone suitable for planning the assassination of Julius Caesar.

Since I had no idea what she was talking about, it was easy to agree I wouldn't let anything slip. Bingo, I thought almost happily. Another suspect. Absently, I stared wondering what I might have observed in the past few days that might prove the Vital Clue.

"This just moves the departmental restructuring up, of course," Carolyn went on, and proceeded to demolish my infant theories and eliminate my major suspect. "Since Davis was leaving us anyway—"

"He was what?" Ice water slopped over the rim of the mug onto my hand.

"Didn't you know? ICF romanced him away—"

"ICF?"

"International Combined Financial Corp. I hear they offered him a real honey of a deal. His next handcuffs weren't going to be golden, they were going to be platinum."

Golden handcuffs, by the way, are those incredible benefits corporations tack onto executive salaries as inducements to stay with the company. Little things like the company Mercedes, the expense account, the stock option, the investment plan. Golden handcuffs. An intriguing term, isn't it?

Carolyn paused, realizing she'd used the wrong tense. "I mean, they would have been. It's too bad."

It's truly amazing how hard it is to remember that someone's dead and won't be back. Ever. It seems so unlikely; the information just won't sink in and stay absorbed.

"Anyway, the whole department's going to be restructured, so . . ." Again Carolyn trailed off, apparently under the theory that we were jolly conspirators together and I also Knew Everything.

"So," I said, and just for something to do, dumped the water out of the mug and then refilled it again. Something thumped against my calf: the spaniel's tail, which never seemed to stop wagging. I stooped down and offered the mug; the spaniel lapped water, regarding me with apparent gratitude.

"So," said Carolyn, pouring herself a cup of Maxwell House, "bye-bye to Davis and his faithful dog Fran. Honestly, you'd think a guy like Davis would want—"

"A more up-to-date model?" I asked with all the acid-laced sweetness a Southern-raised girl can command—which is quite a lot. I suppose it would have been smarter to let Carolyn dish Fran while I kept ferreting for information. On the other hand, maybe it wouldn't have been, and it was too late now.

Because Carolyn had backed off from whatever she'd

been going to say, and changed it to, "But I know she's been with him for years. You don't see loyalty like that much any more. Look, I'll talk to you later; got to run."

Carolyn ran, leaving me standing there with a mug full of cold water, someone else's dog, and a lot of tattered theories. Somehow amateur detection worked out better in mystery novels; I wondered what I was doing wrong.

My mother always did say girls who read too much get into trouble.

The rest of the day was pretty quiet. Brittany Davis's spaniel curled up and slept under my desk while I fielded a lot of phone calls and Fran toiled industriously in the vineyard of what was left of Corp. Res. & Accts. Murder or no murder, quarterly reports must be done—or at least, that was Dayborne's corporate opinion. During a brief lull in the phone calls I'd tried asking Fran about Davis's upcoming move to ICF, which she confirmed, and then began to cry so hard she disappeared into the ladies' room for a full thirty-five minutes. After she came back, I took the little dog for a walk (since it was the Davis dog, I figured it counted as a billable task).

By the time the dog and I returned to the twenty-first floor, Fran was once again engrossed—or pretending to be engrossed—in the quarterly reports. There really didn't seem to be anything else I do could for her but leave her alone with her work, and her grief.

So I kept quiet, and did my own work, and I tried not to wonder about the case any more. This wasn't some intellectual puzzle; a man was dead and someone had very deliberately killed him. I didn't think the murderer had tried to kill Harriet Benson; I thought that was an accident. Poison is not only the coward's weapon, it's the weapon of those who don't care who gets killed.

But how had Harriet gotten some of Davis's coffee—and who could be so cold-blooded as to dump cyanide in it?

You have no idea how amazingly difficult it is to believe that anyone you know—even slightly—could possibly do such a thing. (This is why everyone is always so devastated when a public figure falls from grace; we think we know them. We don't.)

At 4:30, when Brittany Davis *still* hadn't returned, or called, I asked Fran for the Davis phone number. She stared at me as if I'd asked for the Missile Silo Codes; I gently reminded her that we still had Brittany's dog. Grudgingly, Fran told me the number. I jotted it down on a telephone message slip before I dialed. After a counted two-dozen rings, I hung up.

At 5:00, I asked Fran if she wanted to take the Davis dog with her. "It's *her* dog," Fran said in an icy voice, apparently forgetting the dog had been from *him*. "Let her take care of it."

So I sighed mentally and looked down at the spaniel. "I guess you're coming home with me," I said, and the dog wagged her tail for approximately the millionth time that afternoon. She seemed so happy, it was hard not to smile at her.

Silently, Fran and I closed up, and then Fran, spaniel, and I took the elevator down to the glass-and-colonnade main lobby of the building. Most of the ground floor walls are really full-length windows, which is how I knew Lieutenant Kosciusko was waiting outside.

He was leaning against a dark gray Taurus sedan parked in the "No Standing At Any Time" zone right in front of the building. He was wearing faded jeans and a cream-colored river-diver's shirt with the row of little buttons open to bare his neck and the long sleeves pushed up above his elbows.

"Look," said Fran, as we walked out into the summer heat, "it's that policeman."

"Oh?" I said. I was going to add something inane about wondering what he wanted, but before I did he shoved himself away from his car and walked towards us. Slanting afternoon sunlight polished his hair to pure copper.

"Hello, Mrs. Upshaw," he said. "I thought you might like a ride home?" The slight upswing in his voice made it a question. He glanced down at the spaniel, who gazed up at him adoringly and—guess what?—wagged her tail vigorously.

"It's a dog," I said, just in case Lieutenant Kosciusko, trained professional, hadn't realized this fact.

"So I see." He crouched down and held out his hand; the spaniel flung herself at him, wriggling shamelessly as he patted her. Lieutenant Kosciusko apparently didn't worry about getting dog hair on his clothes.

"Did you have some more questions for me, Lieutenant?" I asked, as he stood up.

"As a matter of fact, yes." He sounded just a little sheepish about it. "If you don't mind, of course."

I looked at Lieutenant Kosciusko, and then at the car. "I've got to pick up my daughter," I said.

"No problem. We can swing by there on the way."

"Fine," I said, and turned to Fran, who was standing there in the uncomfortable pose of the person who Doesn't Want to Interrupt or seem to be eavesdropping. "Look, honey, are you all right? Because—"

"I'll be fine," she said. "I've got to go."

"Okay." I admit I didn't question her too hard. "See you tomorrow."

Fran hastened off in the direction of the Whitehall Street

subway stop. I walked with Lieutenant Kosciusko over to his car.

He opened the passenger side door for me, and scooped up the spaniel and placed her on my lap. He closed the door carefully once he was sure I was seated. After he slid in behind the wheel, he flipped the sun visor back up. There was an official looking white card clipped to the front; I read (upside down) "Official Police Business."

"Is it?" I said.

He didn't pretend not to understand. "Well—after a fashion. Seat belt."

"Yes, Officer," I said, and clicked the buckle home. I settled the spaniel upon my lap as the Taurus pulled smoothly into the horrendous death-defying mess that is Lower Manhattan traffic and Lieutenant Kosciusko asked, "What's the address of your daughter's day care?"

"It's at MOP." I gave the address and settled back against the padded seat. Lieutenant Kosciusko turned on the air conditioning and cool air began to blow—as always, right up my ankles and my sinuses. I don't know who designs these things.

"Okay, Lieutenant," I said as the car turned north on Water Street, "ask your questions." For a moment I didn't understand why we weren't just heading straight north on the FDR Drive. Then I realized that bad as the traffic was on the city streets at this hour, it would be ten times worse on the FDR Parking Lot.

"All right." He angled the car sideways, taking it around the angled maze of streets by City Hall. "First, do you mind if I call you Cornelia?"

"To put the suspect at ease? Why, sure," I said, and added, "Victor." It must be nice to have a nice, normal name like that.

"Vic," he said.

"Okay," I said, and then, "Good dog," as the spaniel lifted her head to peer out the window—and did *not* start barking at the pigeons and pedestrians.

"A present for your daughter?" Vic asked, with a swift sidelong glance at the dog.

"A leftover from Brittany Davis. She came, she demanded Davis's checkbook, she departed. Forgetting her dog."

"What's the dog's name?"

"I don't know." I hadn't thought I'd have her long enough to need to know. I began checking the spaniel's rhinestone-laden pink velveteen collar for tags. There weren't any. Oh, well. I gave up, scratched the spaniel behind her long flowing ears, and said, "Are those official questions, Officer?"

"I'm getting to them," he said. "Doesn't Mrs. Davis have her own checkbook?"

"I don't know. What's the next question?"

He shot me a rueful glance. "This one is official—to justify the illegal parking, of course."

"Of course," I agreed, wondering whether Lieutenant Kosciusko preferred my disguise as Mrs. Upshaw, Wonder Secretary or my secret identity as Cornelia, Free—or at least Inexpensive—Spirit. I also wondered why I cared what he thought.

"Anything you want to tell me? Officially, that is?"

"Well—I haven't solved the murder, if that's what you mean."

"It's not," he said. "And please—don't try. Murder's not a game for amateurs."

"But the murder*er*s are amateurs."

"Right. That's why professionals catch them. As I said,

most of the time it's simple, actually." He spoke lightly enough, but he wasn't smiling.

"It's not that simple," I told him ruefully. "Because I had the world's greatest theory this morning at nine thirty and had it blown up into a million pieces at nine forty-five."

"That's par for the course. I didn't say it was easy. Just simple." We were well past City Hall now; Vic turned north again, onto Centre Street. Vic was a good driver, getting where he wanted to go with smooth efficiency and without macho airs and graces. "What was the world's greatest theory, by the way?"

"Oh, that maybe Davis was killed so someone could get his job. But that wouldn't explain Harriet, and it turns out Davis was leaving Dayborne anyway." I explained about how someone (mentioning no names) had offered me a permanent job as his executive secretary.

"Isn't that rather unusual?"

"No, it happens all the time. Good temps get hired out from under their temp agency by companies they're temping for. It's a hazard of the temp business."

"Were you tempted?" Vic was concentrating on his driving; I couldn't quite tell if he was aware of the pun he'd just made or not. A suspicious-minded observer might have thought there was a hint of smile at the corner of his mouth. On the other hand, maybe it was just a shadow.

"Not a chance," I said blandly. "Anyway, I thought that someone might have done it to get Davis's job, but—"

"Nelson Branagh," Vic said, and glanced sideways at me, smiling. "You don't want to get anyone into trouble, which is very commendable. That's a hazard of the police business—but it plays hell with getting evidence."

"So you already know all about it." I felt flattened, and rather cross.

"Well, we know about Davis's new job at something called the International Combined Financial Corporation. Which I suppose is a major heavy-hitter in combined international finance." He sounded faintly baffled; I softened.

"Cheer up, Vic—I haven't the slightest idea what half the places I work for really *do*. And the company names don't help a bit, they truly don't." I could hear myself going all soft and Southern about the vocabulary; I promised myself a good talking-to when I got myself home.

"I see. But do go on—about your train of evidence being derailed."

Since he seemed to really want to hear it, I went on and told him about Carolyn Eaton's conversation, and how she had revealed that Branagh had no motive because Davis was already on his way out Dayborne's heavy glass doors.

"Which doesn't mean Branagh couldn't have done it," Vic interjected. "But motive does help, particularly when the case faces a jury."

"So nobody at Dayborne has a motive?" A thought struck me. "Not a *business*-related motive, anyway. Not one that would explain him *and* Harriet." Harriet's poisoning still seemed more—accidental, somehow. "What about a personal motive?" I demanded.

"We're looking into it, ma'am," he assured me meekly. "Anything else?" He glanced at the dog coiled on my lap. "You mentioned that the widow came by?"

"Yes, Brittany showed up demanding her husband's checkbook. She was pretty riled when Fran and I wouldn't cut the police seal for her. I told her she should ask the police for it, and she scatted out of there, leaving me holding the dog." Hastily, I added, "But she wasn't up there at all Friday."

"You mean, you didn't see her there," he reminded me.

127

The last three blocks to MOP were covered in silence, except for the steady blowing hum of the air conditioning. Lieutenant Kosciusko found a parking space (legal, this time) and pulled into it. Before we got out of the car, he turned to me and said, "Now you see one of the reasons this isn't something you can do as a hobby. You've started to realize that any information you gain may put someone in front of a jury. A person you know. Maybe a friend."

"Maybe I'd be wrong."

"I know. You don't want to get an innocent person in trouble. Well, neither do we. But we do want the person who murdered Davis. I don't want you playing detective— that only works in books. But if you know anything, or even think you do, you have to tell us. We'll sort it out; that's what we're for. We've got the resources to do it, and you don't."

There was a long pause, and I stared out at the people hurrying by on the sidewalk. Not so many people here as farther uptown, and downtown. It was pretty quiet here on East 19th Street. After a moment, Vic got out of the car. He came around and opened my door.

"May I still call you Cornelia?" His voice demanded nothing, awaited my decision.

I knew what he was really asking. I wasn't at all sure I could handle it, but to my surprise I wanted to try. "Yes," I said, and let him help me up out of the car. It being too hot in the summer to leave a dog in the car, the spaniel came along too as we went up to MOP together so I could collect my daughter.

Who set eyes upon the brown-and-white spaniel, shrieked *"DOGGIE!"* and flung her arms around the dog before I could stop her. Not that intervention seemed to be necessary; the spaniel greeted Heather like a long-lost littermate. "*My* doggie!" Heather announced as the dog licked her nose ecstatically, and call it Women's Intuition if you like, but somehow I just knew Heather Melissa wasn't paying any attention to my explanation that the doggie was only visiting for a little while.

"I don't think you've convinced her," Vic said in a voice meant for my ears only.

"Boy, nothing gets past you big city cops, does it?" I said.

And then Vic drove all three of us—me, Heather, and Doggie—home to far East 52nd Street.

Chapter Seven

Thursday Evening

Not being an utter moron about men (despite the claims of some of my nearest and allegedly dearest) I wasn't all that surprised to wind up going out to dinner that night with Lieutenant Kosciusko. Whom I now called Vic. Who had been oddly tentative when he'd asked me for a date.

And who'd left it until almost the last minute to ask. Until, in fact, he'd walked Heather and me upstairs to our own front door, and until I'd opened the door, and Heather had dashed inside, closely followed by Brittany's spaniel, calling for Aunt Lizard. And until I'd thanked him for the ride home, and was just closing the apartment door on him.

"Look," he'd said then, "I don't suppose—"

I pulled the door open again and looked. "You don't suppose what?" I prompted, after a minute, as Vic seemed to have forgotten whatever it was he'd been going to say.

"Look, Cornelia—what are you doing about dinner?" Vic sounded rather abrupt, as if he were Bad Cop questioning a suspect.

For a moment I actually wasted mental energy wondering if supper would stretch to feed a guest tonight. Then my brain cells began functioning more normally and I found myself smiling. "That depends," I said.

"On?" Vic prompted.

Was the damn man going to make me do all the work? Or was this the way nice men acted? Considerate men, who lacked the cosmic certainty that the universe revolved around *them?* Ravenal had never asked, or hesitated; he'd ordered. And for years, I'd dutifully followed orders. . . .

"Vic," I said, cutting to the chase, "are you asking me out to dinner, or inviting yourself to ours?" The moment the words were out, I felt slightly ill, off-balance. My heart thudded wildly.

After a moment, he smiled, looking relieved. "Asking you out," he admitted. "Would you—?"

The question hung between us, unfinished. Behind me, I heard Heather running back down the hall, probably to see what Mother was doing still standing in the doorway. Following Heather came Lizard's slightly louder, slightly slower footsteps. In about three seconds we'd have a fascinated audience. . . .

"Yes," I said hastily. "I would. If Lizard will be home to watch Heather, that is."

Lizard, the dear girl, was delighted to baby-sit in support of such a cause. In fact, she'd practically thrown me into Vic's arms and both of us out of the apartment.

"Now you go *on*, Neely—I can certainly take care of one little old dog, don't worry about a thing, not a *thing*—why, she's just darling and won't be a bit of trouble, and as for your new gentleman, why he's a policeman, so you *know* he's respectable—" Lizard enthused as she pawed through my closet seeking the perfect dress for me to wear.

"Lizard—" I attempted to interrupt this drivel with a dose of cold clear-eyed sanity, without success.

"He's perfect for you," Lizard declared firmly.

This meant I was tall, and so was he. "Liz, leave my clothes alone. I can dress myself, thanks."

"Oh, Neely, don't you have *anything* suitable?" Lizard half-wailed, unimpressed with the contents of my closet.

"And I can't loan you anything, darn it."

"Good. I look like hell in sequins." For once I was glad I wasn't cute and petite like Lizard, because if I had been she'd have been dressing me in one of her Let's Have a Fun Evening outfits right this minute, and I'm just not the fringe-and-glitter type. "Now get out of the way and let me get dressed, okay?"

Reluctantly, Lizard allowed me access to my own closet. *MY* sartorial choice for the evening was a neo-Victorian confection I'd acquired recently on sale at Lord & Taylor's. The dress was Garden Party Posh: blue chiffon printed with opulent pink and white roses; scoop neck framed with a flowing ruffle; mid-calf fluttery skirt.

Lizard approved, grudgingly. Lizard thinks my clothes lack pizzazz. "Want me to do your makeup?" she offered, hopeful to the last.

"No," I said, and began brushing my hair until it haloed my face; a face which looked just fine once I'd touched up my lipstick. I'm ashamed to admit that I chose a romantic rich pink. I never said I was perfect. "And Lizard, *don't* let Heather get the idea that we're keeping that dog."

"She's sure a cute little dog. What kind is she?"

I shrugged, indicating ignorance; I was sure the dog was something purebred and expensive—for one thing, Davis would *never* have given his wife anything less, and for another—well, to quote my maternal relatives, "Good blood tells." The spaniel just *looked* well-bred.

"She looks sort of like a cocker spaniel, but I don't think they've got tails. *No,* Lizard, I am *not* going out on a first date smelling like a Storyville brothel, so put that down."

Lizard shook her head sadly as she set down the perfume bottle; older sisters were a cross to be borne with fortitude and resignation. "Okay, you look great. Now get out there and knock him dead."

I pointed out that this was an unfortunate choice of metaphor, considering that my date for the evening was a Homicide cop.

"Go," Lizard ordered, pointing at the bedroom door.

Sometimes I know when to stop arguing. I went.

Vic had suggested we eat at the little Hungarian restaurant just down the street from my apartment. I'd vetoed that on the grounds (which I did not confide to him) that everyone on the block would know that Cornelia Had A Date within thirty minutes. A girl needs *some* privacy, after all. So after a certain amount of cautious negotiating—you know, finding out whether the other person really, *truly* likes Thai or Italian, or is just too polite to say they loathe your favorite restaurant—we decided on Chinese (the default setting for all New Yorkers in search of dinner) and went downtown to the Phoenix Nest on Second Avenue instead.

And halfway through the appetizers (assorted steamed dumplings; the very nice specialty of the house), Vic asked one of the questions I'd known was coming. "I assume that nice little sister of yours isn't really named Lizard, is she?"

My mouth was full of shrimp dumpling, which gave me a moment's grace. Still, there's no point in trying to keep secrets from a Trained Professional like Vic.

"Lispenard Evangeline," I said once my mouth was empty.

He winced in sympathy.

"And I," I went on with a grim determination to get the worst over with in one blow, "was christened Cornelia Guinevere."

"Well, that's pretty," Vic said. "Old fashioned. Romantic." He smiled. "I like it."

"You," I told him with steely control, "did not spend your high school years being called 'Corny Gwen'." Ah, my dear old high school years in Charleston—years during which I had been tall, gawky, uncoordinated, and, worst of all, smarter than most of the boys, even in math class. My given names were merely Paris Green icing on an already poisoned cake.

"But you can laugh about it now," Vic suggested hopefully.

"Actually," I said, smiling widely, "I can't."

He smiled back, and indicated that the last dumpling was mine if I choose to appropriate it, which I did. "Let me guess—that's why you named your daughter—"

"Heather Melissa." Suddenly uncomfortable under Vic's plainly approving gaze, I transferred my attention to the remaining dumpling. I poked at it with my chopsticks, and wondered why I was here. On a date. I must have been out of my mind.

"Let me guess. Top ten names for girls, both of them," Vic said. "Am I right?"

"Wow, you're the world's greatest detective." When in doubt, apply sarcasm.

"I try," Vic said modestly.

Then General Tso's chicken arrived, and I laughed (lightly, I hoped) and changed the subject—I forget to what. I didn't want to talk any more about my daughter, or her name. I especially didn't want to wind up talking about her father. My late husband. Ravenal.

How could I possibly explain to this nice sane Northerner about the train wreck that had been my marriage? Even I knew that my life with Ravenal had followed the tritest of emotional paths, and that its abrupt ending had been a kind of *deus ex machina* that forever precluded any of what they these days call closure. You can't argue with the dead, and you can't work things out with them.

And it would be nearly impossible to reveal my rash youthful infatuation with Ravenal without making myself sound like a mindless ninny, or to disclose the details of my marriage to him without sounding like a spineless whiner.

As the capper, it would be the height of bad taste to betray just how little sorrow I'd felt at my husband's untimely passing. As I vividly recalled, when the State Trooper, plainly wishing he were doing almost anything else besides breaking the news to a young wife that she was now a young widow, had told me that my husband had been killed in an auto accident, I'd smiled at him and said, "Why, thank you. I'm very much obliged to you." Remarks which, fortunately, had been chalked up to my undoubted deep shock. It had occurred to no one that a woman might be delighted to see the guaranteed last of Ravenal Upshaw.

Oh, I know what you're thinking: that, for heaven's sake, Vic Kosciusko was plainly nothing like Ravenal Upshaw, and that one must Get On With Life. I knew that, and it still didn't help much. It wasn't Vic I didn't trust—it was myself. Having made such a hideous mistake once, I was deeply wary of my own motives and judgment in the area of interpersonal relationships. . . .

"A quarter for your thoughts?"

Vic Kosciusko's voice yanked me back to the present; I discovered I was staring into my water glass as if the ice cubes were a new video game.

"Oh." I uncoiled my fingers from the cool stem of the glass. "Sorry. I was woolgathering."

"Looked like pretty nasty wool."

Vic was regarding me with a certain amount of concern; I shook my head, only partly to clear it. Then I smiled. At least, smiling was my intention.

"Oh, just some old data. Nothing important."

"Look, Cornelia—is this your first date since your husband died?" Now Vic's voice was sympathetic. "Because I know it can be rough—seem disloyal, even—"

"No," I said hastily, "nothing like that." It was only half a lie. First date, yes. Disloyal, no. Rough? That one I'd have to think about more. The way I was going to have to think more about Lieutenant Victor Kosciusko. . . .

As I hesitated, the question I didn't want to ask must have been pretty obvious, because Vic answered it.

"No," he said. "Not me. But I've watched friends who've lost their husband—or wife. It's—not easy." A brief pause, then, "I'm divorced."

His voice was utterly neutral.

"Oh," I said. I turned my wedding ring around on my finger, a nervous habit I developed after Ravenal's death. Then I looked Vic straight in his nice, kind hazel eyes and said, "Do I offer commiseration or congratulations?"

He smiled—rather ruefully, I thought.

"Neither one. It just—happened. It's not easy being married to a cop. After a few years, Roxanne just couldn't take it any more. So—" He shrugged.

Modern day courtship: new pasts for old. Since he'd offered, I was entitled to snoop a bit.

"Any children?"

"A boy. He's with his mother; they live in Denver now."

"Do you get to see him?" Yes, these were pretty personal questions, I suppose—but he'd started it.

"Oh, yes—summers, holidays, that sort of thing. We had what they call an amicable divorce. As divorces go. Would you like to see his picture?"

When I said (of course), that I'd purely love to, Vic grinned at me and pulled his wallet out of his inside jacket pocket. He held the opened wallet out to me, and I leaned carefully over the plate-laden table to regard the little color photo with the requisite admiration.

Vic's son was a sturdy-looking boy whose face was wide across the cheekbones and whose eyes faced the camera with alert dispassionate interest. He seemed, in the photo, to be about ten. His hair was a dark blazing red, although that might be a trick of the studio lighting.

"He looks like you," I said, handing back the wallet. "What's his name?"

"John." Vic smiled again. "Pretty plain, but with a last name like 'Kosciusko', you have to be careful with the first. You appreciate that, I'm sure."

"Believe me, I do—although with us Upshaws, the last name means go wild with the first. It's an old family tradition."

"Which is why 'Heather Melissa'?"

"Which is why 'Heather Melissa'," I agreed. "And you have no *idea* what a family crisis it caused. Why, you'd have thought Sherman was re-burning Atlanta!"

We both laughed (again, lightly—or carefully, take your pick) and Vic caught the waiter's eye and made the scribbling-on-the-palm motion that indicates the check is wanted. And, while waiting for the check to be brought, I sipped ice water and considered the social entertainments we construct for ourselves out of the bitter materials of reality.

The tale of my daughter's naming, for example: a cute story suitable for amusing conversation.

As with so many good stories, most of it's the truth. Not,

of course, the whole truth . . .

As soon as our family knew that Ravenal was dead and that I was to bear his posthumous child, the consensus was that the child, boy or girl, was to be named Ravenal, after his or her dear departed daddy. I didn't bother to disabuse anyone; I left Charleston right after my husband's funeral and was safely in New York, and what was the point of upsetting the whole family? It was bad enough having them all think my Heart Was In The Grave and that I was Prostrate With Grief. I don't know how they explained my immediate flight north to New York City.

The family's horrified enlightenment came in the hospital, where my mother arrived the day after my daughter's birth. (Lizard had timed the call home announcing the arrival of the newest Upshaw belle very carefully. Lizard is a wonderful girl.) Mother cooed over the baby for ten minutes and then said, "I know how hard it is for you, Neely honey, but at least you have Ravenal's dear little baby to console you. Oh, isn't little Ravenal the sweetest thing? You can already tell she'll be just as pretty as her daddy was handsome. A real heartbreaker." (This, by the way, is one of the highest accolades a Southerner can bestow.)

I looked down at the fuzzy little head cuddled in the crook of my arm. Her handsome daddy had wanted her dead—no, not even that. Just—not born. As I watched, she squeezed her kitten-blue eyes closed and yawned. . . .

"She already has a name," I told my mother. "And it sure as hell isn't Ravenal."

While I was pregnant, I had bought half-dozen "name that baby" books, each of which obligingly listed the top fifty names for girls so that you could avoid them. I had studied those lists carefully, and then closed my eyes and pointed twice.

That's how I named my daughter Heather Melissa Upshaw.

It *is* true, as I so gaily told Vic, that this caused a major uproar heard the length and breadth of the Upshaw family tree. To understand this, you must understand that *our* branch of the Upshaws was founded around 1820 by a gentleman named Kennard Berrien Upshaw and his aristocratic English wife, Lady Caroline Darwen. Lady Caroline's *first* husband had been an earl—a *real* earl, his title verifiable in Burke's Peerage. This gives our branch of the Upshaws major points in the Southern Ancestral Sweepstakes (played daily in locations throughout the Old South).

To make sure this aristocratic lineage shall never be forgotten, the successive generations of Upshaw children have been afflicted with such names as Earl, Countess, Lady, and so on, *ad nauseam*. Add to this passion for aristocracy a good dollop of the Arthurian Revival, mix in equal parts of the *Gone With the Wind* mania that still exists in the Southland, and the end result is that our family produces names of more than usual splendor.

The most unfortunate of the current generation is probably my second cousin Letty who was christened, believe it or not, Scarlett Lady Upshaw.

The boys have only a slightly easier time of it. *You* name a boy Ashley Rhett these days and see what happens to him on the playground.

(The acidly-brilliant Southern writer Florence King has dubbed this phenomenon the "I Dreamt I Dwelt In Marble Halls Syndrome"; there is, unfortunately, no twelve-step program to cure it. And if there were, it wouldn't be in time to help sufferers like my brother, Fauntleroy Percival Upshaw. Naturally, this handicap has led to serious macho overcompensation on my brother's part. The last time I heard from Roy, his letter was postmarked Angola.)

The check was brought, and Vic and I both rose to our feet and went to the front of the restaurant toward the cash register. When Vic paid for us both, I nearly demanded to pay my share, but I struggled with myself and for once managed to keep my mouth shut. He'd asked me out; I'd accepted; he was entitled to pay the bill.

The game plan now was to walk back uptown since Vic, having found a legal parking space, had left his car up by my building. A little healthful exercise after eating; I'd been oddly glad to learn Vic liked walking as much as I did.

We squeezed past the giant tank of fancy goldfish making fish-faces at those who entered and left the Phoenix Nest and Vic held the restaurant door for me to precede him out onto the sidewalk. As I went out past him, I heard him sigh faintly. Then we were both standing on the sidewalk in front of the Phoenix Nest's bamboo-tree-with-fabulous-bird painted window and a sleekly handsome black man in a pale beige summer suit was saying, "I'm sorry, Vic, but—"

"But," Vic agreed, and turned to me. By that time I'd recognized Vic's partner, Detective Morton; it didn't take great powers of deduction to figure out that the social part of the evening had come to an abrupt end.

"I'm sorry, Cornelia, but—"

"Murder comes first," I said, quoting Captain William Weigand (fictional creation of Frances and Richard Lockridge).

It is not true that I read only murder mysteries. But in the company of a homicide cop, the mystery genre does seem to take on an added relevance and piquancy.

I could tell Vic recognized the source by the way he smiled. Also by the way he said in a reproving voice, "Now,

Pam." Then he continued, in his normal even tone, "Let me get you a cab first. Charlie, can you flag one down?"

"Don't bother," I said quickly. "I'll walk. It's still early yet. Don't worry; I'll be fine."

"Well," said Vic doubtfully.

"Really," I said, and held out my hand. "Thank you for dinner. It was—" Comfortable; tempting; disturbing? "—lovely," I finished, and we shook hands and Vic went off with Charlie Morton.

I thought I heard Detective Morton say, "For God's sake, Vic—" in exasperated tones just as they got into a plain unmarked car. The slam of car doors cut off the rest of the sentence. The car took off into traffic; a moment later blue lights on the dashboard began to flash and a siren wailed.

I watched until the car disappeared around the corner onto 27th Street. Then I began the walk north to 52nd and home, thinking that Detective Morton had actually done both Vic and me a favor. Police business had scripted the end of our first date; we had been spared the agonizing dilemma of How To End Our Evening.

Unless you've been raised in solitary confinement at the South Pole, you know how that game goes:

Would he try to kiss me? Would I let him if he did? Or—looking at it from the flip side—should he try to kiss me? Would I reject him if he did?

In other words, would he/she think she/he was a jerk if they did/didn't?

Not to mention the delightful new wrinkle that recently has been added to louse up potential relationships: When had either of us last slept with somebody, and had that somebody been a needle-sharing junkie with multiple sexual partners? Or even just the unlucky recipient of a contaminated blood transfusion?

Now you know why so many moderns carry on passionate love affairs with their work.

Furthermore (I told myself firmly), I had sworn absolutely that I was never getting involved with a man again. I was a nice celibate widow lady who lived with her sister and who was devoted to her daughter.

And to her independence. Which I would not risk. Not again—

And just what makes you think Vic Kosciusko wants to kiss you in the first place? I demanded of myself. And myself responded with poisonous sweetness, *Cornelia, honey, don't be more of a jerk than absolutely necessary.*

Myself sounded rather smug about it, too.

When I got home (rather earlier than Lizard and Julian had expected to see me, I suspected), I found out how Detective Morton had tracked down his partner so neatly. Vic had left my number with the central dispatcher; Morton, the need arising, had called it; Lizard had cannily guessed that we'd probably gone to my favorite Chinese restaurant . . . as you see, real Sherlock Holmes stuff.

"You should buy your boyfriend a beeper," Lizard told me, as I tried to convince our visiting spaniel that I was not her Dearest Long-lost Friend in all the wide world. Lizard has a penchant for gadgets.

"For heaven's sake, Lizard, it was only a dinner—yes, you're a pretty girl. One dinner—yes, you're a *good* dog. Sit, damn it! So he could ask me some more questions."

This was not, you will notice, an actual lie, merely a subtle misdirection. Unfortunately, subtlety is wasted on my sister Lizard, just as the "sit" command was wasted on Brittany's dog.

"I'll just bet he did," she said, leering meaningfully.

Julian put one of his long, elegant hands on her arm and said, "Really, Liz," in that beautifully modulated Boston voice of his that makes everyone else sound instantly ill-bred in comparison. Lizard actually flushed, and mumbled that she was sorry.

Julian then proved he was human after all by asking with every appearance of normal curiosity who Lieutenant Kosciusko thought had murdered J. Abercrombie David, as it obviously wasn't me.

"Since if he suspected you, Cornelia, he would hardly have asked you out to dinner. I believe the police aren't allowed to eat or drink with suspects," Julian said.

"I believe you are correct," I replied solemnly. "Really, Julian—he didn't tell me anything." Not about the case, anyway.

"Professional discretion," Julian announced, satisfied. Julian is not, actually, as stuffed-shirtish as he may sound. He's merely morbidly sensitive about everyone else's rights and privileges, and treats everyone with the same formal courtesy he would extend to the Queen of England. This is much more charming than you may think.

"So," I said, looking down at the spaniel, who was more-or-less sitting, tail waving with wild enthusiasm, across my feet, "how'd the dog thing work out?"

"Oh, she's just lovely! Such a sweetie, and *so* well-behaved!" Lizard enthuses better than anyone else I know. "And she just *loves* children! She and Heather look so darling together, I think I'm going to paint them."

"You're not going to have time," I said, "because she's going back to Brittany Davis as soon as I get in touch with her."

"Heather's going to miss the dear little dog," Lizard said.

"Waldo isn't." I felt I was on unassailable ground here, as Waldo, a true egalitarian, hates everything and everybody.

"They're getting on quite well, actually, Cornelia. 'Fighting like cats and dogs' is an exceedingly misleading expression. I don't think you need worry; I'm sure your dog will learn to leave Waldo alone when he hisses at her."

"Julian, she is *not my dog.*" I found myself using the tone required when Heather Melissa intends to wheedle just one more concession out of me before bedtime and I don't intend to indulge her. I made the mistake of glancing down into big round brown spaniel eyes; her flowing ears flattened and she bounced herself a little closer to my legs. "Honey," I told her gently, "you belong to Brittany Davis, and I'll get you back to her tomorrow, okay?"

"Not okay," Lizard began, and Julian touched her arm.

"I think we have time to catch a late showing, Liz. Shall we leave Cornelia in peace?"

Since my non-date with my non-boyfriend had been cut short, there was still a good deal of usable evening left, so Julian and Lizard agreed to go out to the movies. After telling me that Julian had taken our temporary dog out just before I got home, they went off arguing the relative merits of the newest Sly Stallone opus versus *The Terminator*, both playing somewhere downtown. Both Lizard and Julian, gentle beings that they are, enjoy any film in which enough cars, buildings, and/or spaceships are blown to smithereens with the maximum amount of flashy explosions and the minimum amount of reality. When you consider the rather grim social work they both do, this seemingly odd cinematic taste actually makes sense.

I locked up after them and then went in to smooth the covers over Heather, who managed to look like a little sleeping angel, rumpled and innocent. Waldo was coiled beside her, looking like a sleeping basilisk. Waldo doesn't like children, but he does like body heat. Waldo and Heather have developed a mutual non-aggression pact: Waldo knows better than to scratch Heather, and Heather knows better than to pat the kitty.

On my own bed, I found the little spaniel curled up by my pillow. When I approached the bed, her tail began to thump softly against the mattress, and when I reached out, she licked my fingers. "Well, all right," I told her softly, "but it's just for tonight, you know."

Neither child nor cat woke up as I undressed and put on my nightgown. Then I took my silver-backed hairbrush and, followed by the spaniel, went to curl on the padded seat beneath the living room windows. The spaniel sat beside me as I brushed my hair and we both idly watched the dimly lit street. I was catching the breeze through the open windows, and thinking, and I blush to report that my thoughts had damn little to do with the murder at Dayborne Ventures. I thought about policemen a lot, though.

And about me, and my life.

When Ravenal had died, I'd vowed that from now on my life was my own. And my daughter's, of course; Heather would need me until she too grew up. Among the many things I'd sworn to myself was that I wouldn't make the mistake of thinking Heather would remain forever a child.

But Heather was a child now, and I'd also sworn she would grow up in a peaceful, loving home. So what if that home did consist of only her mother and a doting aunt? Better that than a "proper" family—consisting of a repressed half-drunken mother and an immature abusive father.

I'd never considered marrying again—or, rather, I'd considered it and rejected the prospect utterly. Never again. No men; no romantic entanglements. This time, I'd stick to books for my romances. Books were safer than real life. In books, the darkly handsome laughing cavalier of your dreams never lets you down.

The only sensible thing Ravenal'd ever done for me was sign the life insurance policy his employer had provided. Thanks to that, I had a certain amount of money at my back. I also had steady work, and freedom. What more did I want?

Something, part of me insisted—a part I'd thought was dead and buried. *Wrong,* I told myself. *I don't need anything.*

Need, no. Crossly, I brushed my hair harder and told myself I didn't *want* anything more, either. And knew that was a lie; I did want more now. It had been real stupid to go out to dinner with Victor Kosciusko.

Because I liked him, and I didn't want to.

Damn it, I'd had my life beautifully organized—until Lieutenant Victor Kosciusko had walked into it. But I wouldn't let him ruin what I had so painstakingly built. I wouldn't let anything ruin my neat, tidy, beautifully arranged life that was so very unlike my life with the late great Ravenal Upshaw. . . .

As beautifully organized as Fran's life? that rebellious part of me demanded insistently. *As dead as that?*

I try to be at least half-honest with myself. So I sat there in the warm night breeze and continued to brush my hair, and thought about that question real hard.

And after I'd thought for the time it took to brush one hundred slow strokes through my resistant hair, I set my hairbrush aside and pulled my wide gold wedding ring off the third finger of my left hand. For a moment I clutched the ring hard, feeling the band of gold dig into my skin.

Then I opened my hand and tossed the ring out the window. Although it was too dark to see its fall, I thought I heard the little circle of metal land far below. It didn't make much noise. A faint chiming echo in the lamplit darkness; that was all. I looked down into the spaniel's eyes, and decided I saw warm approval in their warm brown depths. I fondled her silken ears, and she licked the air between us as if tasting the summer breeze. "You're right," I said. "Good riddance. Come on, let's go to bed. It's late."

I don't know if it was getting that oddly heavy ring off my finger, or having the little spaniel coiled up against my head (she insisted on sleeping on my pillow), but that night I slept soundly, and didn't suffer any dreams at all.

CHAPTER EIGHT

FRIDAY MORNING

Friday morning I arrived at my desk at Dayborne at a beautifully-timed 8:55. I had considered and rejected the idea of bringing Brittany's dog along; I'd have to make arrangements to return the spaniel today, no matter what Lizard said about a dog not being a lick of trouble and what Heather wailed about wanting a doggie. I had grimly refused to participate in this morning's breakfast game of "What should we call her?" and had *not* bought dog food. The spaniel seemed happy enough to breakfast on Cheerios and eggs and anything else Lizard and Heather dropped accidentally on the floor when they thought I wasn't looking.

When I reached my desk, Fran Jenkins wasn't in sight, but in the center of my clear desktop was a note in her excruciatingly neat handwriting explaining that she'd been called down to Personnel and would I please handle things until she got back. There was a faintly doubtful tone to the note, as if "handling things" might, perhaps, be beyond one person's capabilities.

But aside from answering phone calls—fewer, today, than there had been on Tuesday, Wednesday, and even Thursday—there really wasn't anything much to do. (Oftener than you'd think, there's really not a great deal of office work to do when you're temping for a living; the hiring company wants a warm body filling the vacant chair, but as I've said before, frequently doesn't trust an outsider to do anything much). Unfortunately, Dayborne wasn't the sort of place you could lean back and read at your desk—and yes, there *are* offices like that, trust me; at one such I'd gotten through the entire unabridged Forsyte Saga, from *The Man of Property* to *Swan Song*. At Dayborne, I caught up on my personal correspondence.

So I wrote a long chatty letter to my mother, who rejoices in the name of Magnolia Stuart Upshaw, leaving out everything about murders and policemen, printed the carefully worded document, and put it in my tote bag to mail later. The mail droid trundled around, but I knew better than to put personal mail on it. It probably would be delivered and not waylaid and inspected for Crimes Against the Corporation, but why take foolish chances? I merely walked along beside the mail droid and scooped up the mail for my department.

Oddly enough, Corp. Res. & Accts. seemed to be running along just fine, thank you, without the Big Boss being around—or even alive. The stack of mail was just as thick as usual, and I worked my way swiftly through it, opening and sorting. Condolence letters, apparently to the department in general, on its Tragic Loss. Business letters sent before the sender heard that Davis was dead; I supposed his replacement would deal with them. Interoffice memos regarding such vital aspects of the business as the new hours for the staff cafeteria, automatically generated and sent without regard to their end reader. Half-a-dozen envelopes addressed to Frances Jenkins; I jotted today's date beside her name and set them, unopened, on her desk.

And one long, oddly cheap looking envelope addressed to J. Abercrombie Davis, Executive Vice President. Sensory memory is a wonderful and a terrible thing; the feel of the envelope's paper on my fingertips reminded me of the last time I'd handled such a missive, and so I got a Kleenex out of my drawer and used it to protect the letter within the envelope from my fingers and their prints and skin oils. Nor was I in the least surprised to pull out a sheet of white typing paper and unfold it to read that *You Will Be Sorry Someday! ! !*

The words had been cut from a newspaper and taped to the paper, as had the three exclamation points. The three exclamation points were three different sizes. The anonymous author must have had to search to find enough for suitable emphasis. "I know the Post Office delivers things late," I told the threatening letter softly, "but this is a bit ridiculous." The intended recipient was already "late"—later than the letter could ever be.

I looked the letter over carefully, and then equally carefully slid it and its envelope into a manila folder. I was about to phone Vic—er, Lieutenant Kosciusko—when the phone rang. A quick double ring: interoffice. I picked it up before the second double ring. "Corporate Restructuring and Accounts, Mrs. Upshaw speaking."

"Cornelia?" It was Amber, the receptionist. "Is Fran there?"

"No, she isn't, so I'm afraid you will have to make do with me." Maybe I *do* read too much. However, Amber didn't recognize the Saki quote, so I suppose it didn't matter.

"Well, look, there's a guy out here demanding to see Davis. I told him he was dead, but he wants to see somebody anyway. Maybe he thinks I'm joking him or something. *I* don't know."

I didn't bother to sort out Amber's pronouns, simply saying, "I'll be right out." I hung up and went down the hall and out through the big glass doors into the receptionist's lobby on twenty-one.

150

Amber sat coolly behind her Starship Enterprise sweep of desk-and-all-mod-high-tech-cons; she was keeping under observation, with apparent politeness, a rather rumpled-looking man in a not particularly good suit. It had obviously not been purchased at Barney's, emporium of choice for up-and-coming middle management.

As I came out, Amber looked at me and rolled her eyes meaningfully. A problem, this; one Amber was happy to bump upstairs to the next level.

"Good morning," I said. "I'm Mrs. Upshaw. May I help you?"

Our visitor stared at me. He looked about thirty, and rather wild-eyed, with a positively Cassian lean and desperate look. "You're not Fran," he announced.

"I'm sorry; Fran is away from her desk right now." The all-purpose office excuse, covering everything from "she's right there but wouldn't talk to *you* for a million dollars in 1963 currency" to "she's skipped out with her lesbian lover and a biker gang and won't be back until after the six o'clock orgy." Usually, of course, it's the polite way of saying someone's in the bathroom. "Can you tell me what this is about? Maybe I can help you."

"This girl says Davis is *dead*. Is that true?" He sounded hopeful, horrified, and suspicious all at once; an unpleasant combination of emotions.

"Yes, I'm afraid it is." I considered the visitor curiously. It was certainly possible this man might not know Davis was dead. After all, Davis's death—murder or not—hadn't exactly been front-page news. Maybe the police were keeping the information of the crime under wraps. Or maybe this little murder just wasn't flashy enough to compete with the celebrity divorce scandal-of-the-week, the rescue of half-a-dozen girls from a homemade dungeon in Queens, and the

151

gang shoot-out in Times Square.

"Good," said the man under his breath. At least, that was what I thought he said. He may, of course, have muttered, "Great."

"Yeah," Amber put in helpfully. "I told you he was dead. Like, he was murdered—we had the police here and everything."

"Murdered," the man whispered. Apparently he hadn't expected that word to surface in the conversation. Now he sounded truly appalled, and seemed to turn faintly green about the mouth. Then he managed a slight recover, struggling for nonchalance.

"Look—Ms. Ur—" Now he sort of smiled with an obvious effort, producing the facsimile of an expression meant to be friendly and confiding. "Davis has a couple of—of things of mine. I don't suppose I can go in and get them?" Here he actually laughed, in a ha-ha fashion that wasn't at all convincing.

"I'm sorry, but the police still have his office sealed, Mr.—?"

The trick didn't work; he didn't tell me his name. In fact, he didn't say anything for a moment, just stared at me. I thought that he didn't look at all well.

Inspiration and idiocy struck at the same moment, with equal force. "What won't Mr. Davis get away with?" I asked in a conversational tone. "And why is he going to be sorry?"

Mr. X turned even paler and backed away from me as if I'd suddenly turned into Count Dracula and was about to sink my fangs into his neck. Which I suppose, metaphorically speaking, I already had.

"How—I don't know what you're talking about." His voice quavered.

Real convincing.

"If you didn't kill him, you should tell the police about the letters you wrote to Mr. Davis before they come asking you about them," I went on. "Or even if you—"

I was talking to empty air and Amber. Our nervous visitor took off while I was in the middle of my helpful advice. He rocketed out the heavy glass doors to the elevator lobby. I followed, to observe only; he pushed frantically at the elevator button, cast an anguished glance at me, and then spotted the door to the fire stairs. He yanked the door open and fled through it. By the time I got over there, all I could hear was footsteps echoing off the concrete stairs several flights below.

I didn't follow him—I'm not *that* big an idiot. I closed the fire exit door again and went back into the Dayborne lobby. "Amber, when that guy was here, did he give a name at all?"

"Nope. You know what they're like."

"Listen, did he touch anything while he was waiting? The desk, a magazine, anything?"

"Gee, I don't know. He just stood there fidgeting, you know?" Amber was staring at me wide-eyed. "You think *he's* the guy did it?"

"I don't know. If he comes back, let me know right away, okay?"

"You got it," Amber said fervently. "What're you going to do now, Cornelia?"

"Call the police," I said, which I had the feeling disappointed Amber. It seemed so tame, somehow.

Tame, but sensible.

When I got back to what was left of Corp. Res. & Accts., Fran was back from Personnel. She was sitting at her desk, straight-backed and rigid, with a face like stone.

"Fran?" I said gently.

"They've let me go," Fran said.

Which meant, translated into plain brute English, that Dayborne had fired her. There wasn't much to say, but I said it anyway. "Oh, Fran, I'm so sorry—"

"I won't say," Fran went on in a perfectly flat voice, "that I didn't expect it. They're being quite generous, really. A month's severance pay. And of course paying for all my sick leave and vacation."

"Oh, Fran honey." I went over and put my arm around her shoulders; I'm not sure she noticed. God damn it, you'd think Dayborne would have *some* use for a secretary with thirty years experience and flawless typing.

"It's not easy to get another job at my age, you know," she went on.

"Look Fran, honey, you've been working hard all your life. Maybe you'd like to retire now? Relax, enjoy yourself?"

But I couldn't imagine her enjoying herself, either. I thought of her lifeless apartment—not even a plant to keep her company. With Davis dead, her career as his dedicated assistant—her reason for being—was also dead. Now she was as bereft of hope and purpose as any other widow.

Fran began aimlessly shifting papers from one neat pile to another. Back and forth the papers went, Fran's hands moving as steadily as the hands of a particularly reliable clock. *This isn't fair,* I complained fiercely to the universe. *First her beloved boss is killed, and now she gets fired.*

"They're restructuring, and they haven't any place for me, you see." Fran looked up at me, and her eyes seemed dull, unseeing. "I hear they want you, though. Congratulations."

"Well, I don't want them," I said, and Fran just stared at me as if I were mad, or from Mars. After a moment, I thought of something useful to suggest. "Fran, what about trying ICF? I know Davis and you were going there. Maybe—"

"Nobody will want me without him. We were a team." This last was said with a brief flare of pride.

"I'm sure that's not true. You're a fabulous secretary, any company would be lucky to get you." Then I had a real brainstorm. It was perfect; it would solve everything. "Look, Fran—why don't you come work temp for MOP? They'd purely love to have you."

I heard my voice warm with genuine enthusiasm; this was a wonderful idea! Metropolitan Office Professionals *would* love to have Fran—her skills, her experience, her loyalty. And I wouldn't mind the bonus I'd get for bringing in a new MOP employee.

"MOP is absolutely terrific to work for, and—"

Slowly, Fran seemed to focus her eyes on me. "Work as a *temp?*" she said, the same way you'd say, "Work as a 42nd Street *hooker?*"

I recoiled, staring at her. After what seemed a very long time, I thought, *Why, Fran doesn't like me. How odd.* An instant later, I thought, *How rude,* which still seemed sort of inadequate. Then I felt anger rising hot and rash, and knew I was about to say something I'd have a hard time forgiving myself for later—

Thank God, the phone rang then. My phone, so I could leave Fran and run over to my desk to answer it. Long, steady single rings: outside call.

"Good morning; Dayborne Corporate Restructuring and Accounts. May I help you?" My voice was admirably steady.

"Is this Cornelia Upshaw?"

"Vic! I'm glad you called." Now I remembered I'd been

just about to call the police when Fran's problems had side-tracked me. Forcing down my anger, I hastily recounted the Tale of the Anonymous Young Man and his no-longer-so-anonymous letters.

Vic was admirably professional, getting full details and my description of Mr. X. When I suggested the police fingerprint the receptionist's area, though, he was doubtful that it would help.

"Without printing everyone at Dayborne, we couldn't be sure we'd gotten his prints—unless he's already on file somewhere. Probably not worth the time and effort."

"Oh. But—"

"But we do appreciate the information. I'll pass it along." He also suggested I come down and work up a picture of the visitor with one of the department's artists.

"Of course," I said. "Should I come down this afternoon?"

"Could you? It would be very helpful." Vic sounded oddly remote: his professional voice.

"I don't see why not. There's nothing to do here anyway." I said this deliberately, without looking over at Fran.

"Fine," Vic said, and told me what address to go to, and who to ask for. "Tell them I sent you over in regard to the Davis case."

"Okay," I said, scribbling down his instructions on the nearest memo pad. Then I remembered that *he'd* called *me,* and I'd hardly let him shove a word in edgewise. "Oh, I'm sorry, Vic; I should have asked—what were you calling me about?"

There was the briefest of pauses; a delay just long enough to clue me that something was wrong. That whatever Vic was going to say next, I wouldn't like.

"Look, Cornelia—"

Vic proceeded to explain to me, as tactfully as he could, that he'd been out of line when he asked me to dinner the previous day. That, since I was involved, however peripherally, in the case he was investigating, professional decorum proscribed a social relationship.

So that was why Vic had called me. For some reason, I wasn't entirely surprised, and then I realized why. As Vic spoke, trying to explain, I remembered those half-heard, exasperated words from Detective Morton: *"For God's sake, Vic—"* I suspected now that the words ending that sentence had been, *"Are you out of your mind?"*

"Until the case is over, of course," Vic finished up. "I hope you understand." Another pause. "May I call you then?"

On telephones, there is only the voice to judge by. Vic's voice was being carefully controlled: level and a little flat. But there was an undertone of resignation, the faintest hint that he expected, inevitably, that I would not understand. That his request would be refused—refused, probably, with great hurt and indignation on my part.

And I admit my first response was hurt and indignation. Here I'd peeled back some of my armor, laid my emotions out to be played with, and now he backed off, pleading his profession—why, how dare he, after I'd already made my big emotional gesture!

Pretty silly, right? I thought so too; I found myself smiling. And I also found myself considering the flattering fact that Lieutenant Victor Kosciusko had been so enthralled by Cornelia Upshaw's charms that he'd ignored the warning voice of his saner, more professional self.

Mind, I didn't think Vic would have taken me to dinner if he'd seriously thought I was a suspect. *That* would have been stupid, and Vic was not stupid. *This* was romantic, in a sensible sort of way.

"Cornelia?" Vic sounded truly resigned, now.

"Of course I understand," I said. "Call me as soon as you can. Oh, and Vic—tell Detective Morton he was absolutely right."

"Not entirely," said Vic, and his voice sounded completely different now, once more placidly amused. "Thank you, Cornelia."

"Any time, Lieutenant," I told him, and hung up, feeling oddly pleased with both myself and Vic.

I looked over at Fran, who was pointedly Not Paying Any Attention to me or my telephone conversation, and told her I was going up to police headquarters. Fran didn't seem to care much one way or the other. Mentally shrugging her off, I filled in my timesheet, indicating I was leaving early (which meant losing a few hours' pay today, but Civic Duty must be done). Then I got my purse out of the desk drawer, locked up, and went lightheartedly off.

CHAPTER NINE

FRIDAY AFTERNOON—AND EVENING

The police department was both fascinating (see our tax dollars at work; crimes solved while-you-wait) and boring (and wait, and wait, and wait . . .).

By the time I caught a taxi and got up to Police Plaza, it was lunchtime, so half the people were Out To Lunch and the other half were overworked. Rather than spend an hour prowling through labyrinths of dingy beige halls and scuffed marble floors, I went out, found a vendor with a shiny new blue-and-yellow Sabrett's umbrella on his stand, and bought a hotdog with mustard and sauerkraut and a Coke. Lunch *al fresco,* New York style.

When I had finished eating lunch, I went back in to the massive glass-and-concrete maze, finally found the right department, gave my name, rank, serial number, dropped Vic's name, and waited some more. Fortunately I almost always carry a book with me, because staring at dingy bilious-green walls definitely palls after five minutes. The waiting area walls were decorated with numerous posters, warnings, and notices that might have been amusing to read, but I found myself reluctant to wander and draw attention to myself.

So I sat quietly on the long waiting room benches, in the company of a lot of other people who were also waiting. Each of us passed the time until we were summoned to our respective destinies in our own way. Some people read newspapers or flipped through magazines. Some crocheted, or wrote letters, or filled in crossword puzzles, or scolded restive children. One enterprising young woman was painting her nails in alternating stripes of international orange and metallic blue. Most people just stared at the walls, apparently fascinated by the City of New York's amazing use of color in public buildings. I tried to read my book, but it was difficult to concentrate on the printed page. Police headquarters is simply not a comfortable place to sit, even if your conscience is clear. The unpadded wooden benches don't help.

After I'd apparently waited enough, I got to sit in a small greenish room instead of a large one. There a quick-sketch artist asked me lots of questions and kept erasing lines and saying, "More like this, you mean?" until I agreed that, yes, that looked more like Mr. X of the Anonymous Letters than it didn't. It was fascinating, all right, but a lot more difficult and much more tiring than I'd thought it would be. Thinking is hard work.

Then they asked me if I'd please Make A Statement, which I did. I was then told that I'd been Very Helpful, Ma'am, and allowed to find my way back into the invigorating summer air.

Lower Manhattan during a June heat wave is no place to loiter. I looked around to get my bearings, looked at my wristwatch, and headed for the nearest pay phone. First I called MOP's day care to tell them what they'd already figured out for themselves: that I'd be late picking up Heather. Fortunately that wasn't a problem, since MOP day care stays open for extended hours to accommodate working world exigencies. Which is sometimes a real lifesaver, but I still don't like being late when I'm picking up my daughter.

"Message for you from Holly," the day care receptionist

chirped in the MOP-approved friendly and helpful fashion. (MOP sometimes trains temps by hiring them in-house to staff the offices and day care center.) "Just a sec—oh, yes—your current assignment would like you to please come back and work overtime tonight. Is that okay?"

I thought about the request for a few seconds. I, a normal human being, couldn't imagine what project required urgent overtime now that the department head was dead. On the other hand, Dayborne was not a normal human being, and neither were its multitudinous vice presidents. On the third hand, while this last-minute routine was a real pain, maybe the Corp. Res. & Accts. department actually was in a real bind this time. By Monday, I fully expected Dayborne Ventures Inc. to have finished "restructuring" itself and be smoothly continuing its appointed tasks with Nelson Branagh, EVP, in control. But Branagh hadn't taken up the reins yet, and Davis had run his little corner of corporate heaven with an iron fist; without him in charge, chaos might very well be reigning. . . .

After paying *danegeld* to a computerized voice that demanded another quarter for the next three minutes, I told the MOP receptionist that yes, tonight's unexpected stint was okay—"*If,*" I added darkly, "I can get my sister to pick up my daughter. I'll call you back."

Lizard was home; Lizard would pick up Heather. "And we'll take Flopsy for a walk over along the river."

"We are *not calling her Flopsy,*" I said, realizing only after I hung up that I should have said, "We are *not keeping that dog!*" But that was another problem, to be dealt with later. Now I called MOP back and told Jennifer that I would Go The Extra Mile (as the corporate types are real over-fond of saying) and work the overtime. "At least Dayborne's air conditioned," I said, as I assured MOP (represented by the perky Jennifer of the day care center) that I would indeed return unto Dayborne.

As I hung up, having spent sixteen minutes by the clock monopolizing the phone booth, I made a note to tell Holly Steinberg that I wanted a low-key non-corporate placement after this one. Some of us have lives to live.

Having struggled back to Dayborne through June heat and lower Manhattan rush hour traffic, I arrived there at 5:45 and was pretty damned ticked off to discover that the urgent overtime simply involved collating a bunch of inter-office reports that I could have finished that morning if anyone had bothered to give them to me. I mentioned this.

"I forgot," said Fran.

This struck me as a little odd. But I was all hot and cross and bothered, and, frankly, I didn't pay that much attention. So Fran had forgotten; the poor thing had a lot on her mind. So sue her.

Fran went back to industriously finishing up whatever One Last Thing had kept her here past 5:00. Typical of Fran; utter devotion to duty—and to Davis, even though he was no longer around to appreciate her talents. I thought, cattily, that Fran was a bad example to us all. Then I was ashamed of myself.

It was oddly quiet for Dayborne, which frequently didn't run out of steam until 7:00 or so, and it wasn't quite 6:00 yet. But hyperactive corporate culture notwithstanding, today most of the employees seemed to have headed home already; only the diehards were working this evening.

Fran typed, staring intently at handwritten copy resting on her typing stand. Unlike most modern typists, she never glanced at either her fingers or the computer viewscreen.

Her fingers danced over the keys while her eyes remained fixed upon the copy she was transforming into a word processing document.

I collated, and wondered if Vic *would* really call me, once the investigation into Davis's murder was wrapped up. Actually, I didn't really wonder that too hard. Mostly I wasted quite a lot of time in an in-depth consideration of every conceivable reaction I could possibly have when I saw Vic next.

This mental activity gave me a very peculiar unsettled feeling in the pit of my stomach. After Rav, I'd sworn off romance. Sworn I would never again give a man the chance to take away my freedom and my self-respect.

I certainly wasn't about to hand myself over to Lieutenant Victor Kosciusko—even assuming he'd want such a dubious gift. And what made me think he would? A common interest in a murder was not enough to base a relationship upon. We'd been on precisely one date, and here I was already developing a rich, full emotional life. Vic probably wouldn't call anyway. . . .

Even I couldn't make myself believe that—and I realized that I didn't want to. So I settled for worrying over more mundane questions, such as:

What should I wear?

How should I do my hair?

Was I out of my mind?

Collating (taking one item from each of several stacks and putting them together in order to form the complete document or packet) is repetitive, mindless, soothing work; I've done some of my best thinking while collating. This was not some of my best thinking, but it was nevertheless amusing, in a quiet way.

Fran finished off her typing, closed up her area, and left

at 6:30. "Oh, by the way," she said, "when you've finished that, Ms. Eaton wants you to do some typing for her."

Typical; once you've agreed to stay late, you're usually trapped for the duration. I sighed, and tried to care about all the lovely overtime I was earning. "Where is it?"

"She'll bring it out when it's ready," Fran said. "Here's the memo she left you."

I took the paper and watched Fran walk down the corridor to the exit doors. She seemed to move heavily, the weight of worlds pressing her down. At the doors she looked back at me. "There's fresh coffee in the pot," she called back.

"Thanks." I waved absently, thinking that Fran really ought to get herself some rest, and glanced down at the memo from Carolyn Eaton. Like Carolyn herself, the memo was crisp, clear, and to the point:

> *Cornelia—I'll have some minutes for you to type later this evening. I need them for tomorrow morning. Thanks for waiting.*

The memo was signed with the bold slashing initials Carolyn used on all intra-office correspondence. A power signature; one Carolyn had probably carefully designed and practiced.

At least she'd said thank you.

The collating was finished at 7:00. I looked at the time, and then down the hall to Carolyn Eaton's office, and sighed. After a moment, I went and tapped on her door. "Ms. Eaton?"

No answer. "Minutes" meant a meeting, which could be held anywhere, but apparently wasn't being held in Carolyn's office. So I went back to my desk, pulled out my lunchtime book (*Time-Tranced Bride* by Arden Frost, a lush, lurid romance about a lovely yet spirited lady with a Past— or possibly a Future—and a handsome yet mournful bucca- neer with a Secret Sorrow; as you may perhaps have de- duced, I do not only read mysteries), and settled down to wait. I couldn't quite face *Can You Forgive Her?* and its teeny type after the day I'd had—and twice couldn't face Alice Vavasor's endless vacillation between steady John Grey and rakish George Vavasor.

Odd, you think? I should have suspected something, you think? Then all I can say is that you aren't very familiar with major corporations. Or even some minor ones, for that matter. Let me tell you a professional secret: executives think *your* time is worth nothing, even to you.

Trust me, nothing was more likely than that Carolyn Eaton, overachieving AVP extraordinaire, doing not only her own job, but that of Harriet Benson, still hospitalized ditto, had left a message for me to wait and then gone off into a meeting somewhere. From which conclave she would eventually emerge, make a casual and insincere apology for keeping me waiting, and then toss at least three hours' worth of typing onto my desk. And then be hurt and sur- prised if I didn't want to stay there until midnight and type the stuff. With a smile on my face and a song in my heart, too.

Oh, and don't forget to be in promptly at 9:00 the next morning, okay?

By 7:30 the only sounds I heard on the twenty-first floor were the air circulating and the office machines humming to themselves. Most of the other late-working staff had left. I set down my romance and went padding around to check out the territory.

Neither the big conference room nor the small conference room was in use, which meant Carolyn's meeting could be anywhere, including in another company in another building. Down the hall and around the corner two people were working feverishly over a computer. Past them I saw the reassuring brown of the uniformed guard; Nottingham Security patrols Dayborne after 6:00.

I made a brief stop in the staff lounge, considered and rejected the coffee Fran had mentioned. By this time it was undoubtedly overcooked and stale, and I have a limited tolerance even for good coffee. Not to mention that, somehow, I just couldn't summon up much enthusiasm for the coffee at Dayborne any more. I killed some time pouring out the old coffee and washing the pot before I went back to my desk. I wished there were something as plebeian as a soda pop machine in the staff lounge so I could relax with a nice cold Coca-Cola. It would be even nicer if I could mix some bourbon with it.

Seven forty-five, and still no sign of Carolyn. Irritation took over, preventing me from concentrating on my book. But I was too twitchy to just sit and do nothing.

So I created a flyer. When I was finished playing with the typeface fonts, I displayed my work in the "view document" mode and saw that it was good. I used the laser printer to run off half a dozen copies of the flyer on some bright pink paper I found in the back of the bottom drawer of my desk and went around thumbtacking the flyers on the "Staff Information" centers (authorized material only may be placed on these bulletin boards). The flyers announced that

LACK OF PLANNING ON YOUR PART DOES
NOT CONSTITUTE AN EMERGENCY ON MINE

What could Dayborne do, after all, even if they found

out I was the one who had perpetrated this outrage? Fire me?

It was now 8:45. Beyond the sweeps of plate glass window at the ends of the hall it was dark—or as dark as it ever gets in the city that never sleeps or turns out its lights. I gave Carolyn Eaton one last chance (after all, whatever she wanted might, actually, be really important); I went down to her door and knocked again. Hard. No answer, and when I tried the knob, I found the door was locked.

Suddenly I spooked; it was late, and I was almost alone on the floor, and I started imagining Carolyn lying there over *her* desk. Dead like Davis, waiting with eternal patience to be found—

The security guard I eventually persuaded to open Carolyn's door was pretty disgusted with me. "See, lady? Nothing here. Okay?"

He was right; Carolyn's office was perfectly empty and composed: papers stowed away, desk clear, files locked. Her computer was powered off, and the keyboard had been removed and locked up somewhere. (Security again.)

Carolyn not only wasn't there, alive or dead, but she had obviously gone home quite some time ago.

The guard backed me out of Carolyn's office and relocked the door. "Look, lady, it's late. Why don't you go home or something?"

"I sure will," I told him fervently. I thought of leaving Carolyn's memo to me in the middle of her nice clean desk, stapled to one of my bright pink flyers, but that would be petty. And her door was already locked again, anyway.

Back at my desk, I shook my head over Carolyn's memo asking me to stay and dumped it into my top desk drawer. Monday I'd confront her with this evidence of her perfidy, and hope she'd at least be good and sorry that Dayborne would be paying me overtime for nothing. Then I called the cab service Dayborne used and told them to pick up ASAP. I noted the time I left (9:10, and I was going to get paid for every last minute and portion thereof I'd spent at Dayborne that evening it if it killed MOP getting it) and stalked out of there so mad I could hardly see straight.

As I passed the door to Davis's office, which was still criss-crossed by police tape, I distinctly recall thinking that it was a real shame more executives didn't drop dead.

At least I had the faint consolation of knowing that Dayborne was going to pay for my cab, damn its incorporated eyes.

Traffic was light until we reached 51st Street. There we encountered such a snarl of vehicles that I told the cab driver to let me off half a block away from the corner of my street. I tried not to slam the cab door when I got out. I was still fuming when I reached the corner of First and 52nd and turned right.

Never walk city streets when you're too mad to see straight.

I was so absorbed by my anger that I didn't really notice what I was passing, or who. It was almost a surprise to realize that I had reached my apartment building.

In fact, I was already three steps into the outer courtyard leading to the main entrance. The evergreen-shrub-lined, badly lit central court seemed darker than usual tonight. Darker, and the night shadows somehow menacing. . . . Suddenly I stopped, uneasy.

I don't know what made me think something was wrong. Nothing moved in the dimness, and the only sound was the steady drip of water in the little fountain. Above me win-

dows shone warmly gold, or flickered uncanny blue if a television set was on. I heard the whir of air conditioners from
some of the windows, and an unintelligible blend of human
voices and warring musical styles from others.

But something was not quite right. In the city, as in any
other jungle, you develop finely-tuned senses that let you
stay alive. Sight, sound, scent—your subconscious learns to
analyze what you don't know you've seen, and produces its
conclusions as the hunch that holds you waiting where you
can see the token booth instead of moving down the plat-
form. Or as the impulse that sends you crossing to the other
side of the street. Ignore this information at your peril.

Tonight I nearly did ignore that warning inner voice.
The building entrance was less than a hundred feet away,
and I had an overactive imagination.

I even took two more steps into the courtyard—and suddenly I knew I could not walk through that shadowlit dimness to get to the front door.

But I'd be damned if I'd start yelling over nothing and
get everyone in the building all upset. Slowly I backed up
into the street and checked around. I was the only pedestrian on the block of course, and most of the shop windows
were dark. All except one. I headed for Mirror, Mirror.

Although the sign in the door of Mirror, Mirror said
"Closed," lights still shone behind the glass. I leaned on the
bell hard until Rue peered out and instantly opened the
door.

"Cornelia? What happened? Are you all right?" Rue
reached out and hauled me inside, slamming the door behind me and throwing the locks with swift efficiency.

"Nothing happened; I'm fine."

It wasn't until I tried to convey this information that I
realized how shook up I was; I was gasping for breath and

169

my heart was pounding so hard I could hear it beat.

"You sure?"

Rue regarded me with worried skepticism. I could tell she was just itching to mother me, given half a chance. Rue is a real nice lady, fortyish and pretty in a Rubenesque way. She's definitely the motherly sort, which makes what happened to her even worse. Once she'd been like me: working simultaneously on the perfect marriage and a nervous breakdown.

Unlike me, she'd found consolation in religion. In her case, goddess worship, which is the up-and-coming thing here in the Big Apple but didn't go over real well back in Flyover Country. Indiana, I think she said once.

The upshot in her case was a real nasty divorce; her husband got both kids and a restraining order. Rue got to leave the state with her skin intact. Now she manages Mirror, Mirror, selling crystal balls and tarot cards and books on religion and the occult. She'll never see her kids again, unless she can track them down after they turn eighteen.

It seemed to me that her Goddess hadn't done any better for Rue than my God had done for me, but unlike me, Rue was still optimistic about the relationship. (I'd walked out of Grace Church, the finest Episcopalian house of worship in Charleston, in the middle of Reverend Hamilton's fulsome eulogy to my late husband and hadn't looked back since.)

"Cornelia, are you sure you're all right?" Rue repeated. "Should I call the police?"

I shook my head, and started to apologize. I was already beginning to feel like the ultimate idiotic hysterical female. Rue wasn't having any of that.

"Don't be silly, Cornelia; you did just what you should." She smiled, and her big brown eyes didn't look quite so worried any more. "Come on—how many times have we said more women should have the courage to risk acting like a jerk?"

"I know—but this time *I'm* the jerk," I said.

I almost managed to convince myself. But not quite, because, by accident, my life had crossed a murderer's. I didn't know the murderer, but he—or she—knew me.

And thought I knew more than I did? And been waiting for me? Or had there just been a random mugger lurking in the shadows—or had there been nothing there at all?

"Well, you're not walking home alone—that's what neighbors are for, remember?" Rue picked up the phone and punched a number with brisk efficiency.

"Oh, Rue, really—"

"Shut up," Rue instructed out of the side of her mouth, so I wandered about the shop, absently looking at books and New Age knickknacks while Rue talked. "Great," she finished. "We'll wait."

She hung up and said to me, "Five minutes. Matt's coming by for you. Now *don't* start apologizing again, or I'll make you buy a book, and you and Lizard don't have *room* for another book."

So I waited meekly until Matt arrived. And, to be perfectly frank, I greeted him with great relief. Matt Richmond's a big black guy: about six-foot-five and built like Darth Vader. He lives in the top apartment of the brownstone right across the street from Mirror, Mirror, and he's an orthopedic surgeon at New York Medical Center. In his spare time he rebuilds old motorcycles.

Like Rue, Matt brushed away my apologies, told me I'd done just what I should, and escorted me back to my building. Walking with Matt makes a girl feel Real Secure. Nothing happened on the way, of course; anyone who'd been in the courtyard was long gone, if anyone had ever been there at all.

Matt accompanied me inside and up to my apartment door. As I turned the key in the Medico, I heard barking from the other side of the heavy door. "New dog?" Matt asked, and I shook my head.

"No, I'm just keeping it for a—" I balked at calling Brittany Davis a "friend," so I settled for, "—an acquaintance." The barking was now just the other side of the door, which I opened hastily. The spaniel instantly flung herself at Matt and me as if we were her long-lost parents.

"Cute Cavalier." Matt crouched down and allowed the dog to writhe herself about him in a truly extravagant fashion. White dog hair clung to his dark slacks. "Needs a good brushing out," he added, with a glance at his clothes.

"A cute what?" I tried to grab the little dog, and managed to catch her up in my arms. She promptly started washing my face.

"She's a Cavalier King Charles Spaniel," Matt said, and scratched the dog behind one of her luxuriantly flowing ears. "My sister has one. What's her name?"

"I don't know. We thought she might be part Cocker Spaniel—but the person who owns her would never own a mutt."

"Well, she's not a mutt, she's a Cavalier. Didn't your acquaintance mention that?"

"Well, actually—no." I hastily regaled Matt with the story of how I'd come to have temporary—with a heavy accent on the *very* short-term nature of the informal arrangement—custody of the little dog. "She's going back tomorrow," I finished, and Matt smiled.

"Right," he said, and fortunately before I could respond to his patent disbelief, Lizard appeared at the other end of the hallway. She hovered for a moment, plainly prepared to tactfully vanish again, until she saw Matt. Then she ran down the hall to the door, demanding to know what had happened.

"Neely? Are you all right? I heard Crumpet bark, but then I heard you open the door, and I thought you'd want to say goodnight to your policeman without an audience, so—"

"Lizard, I'm fine, we are not calling her Crumpet either, because she's not our dog and we're not keeping her, and Vic is not *my* policeman." I didn't dare look at Matt. Fortunately, unlike some people I could mention, Matt is discreet, as befits a physician.

"I'd better let you two work this out," Matt said, and after I thanked him profusely, and he assured me it had been no trouble at all, I allowed Lizard to haul me inside and close the door.

"Okay, Neely," Lizard began, only to be interrupted by Matt calling through the door, "Now let me hear those locks, ladies."

Since my arms were full of spaniel, Lizard obediently turned the key lock and then shot the deadbolt.

"Chain," Matt demanded.

"I'm getting it, I'm getting it." Lizard rattled the chain into its slot. "Satisfied now?" I called.

"Okay," Matt said, and I heard, faintly, his footsteps as he jogged down the stairs.

"Now, Neely, you're going to come in and sit down and tell me what happened," Lizard ordered, and I sighed, realizing I was going to have to explain the entire non-event once more. Nor was Lizard distracted by learning what kind of dog we had visiting us. No, she insisted on hearing the entire tale of my by now seemingly endless Dayborne day.

At least it was the last time that night I had to tell the story, because after I had repeated it for what now seemed the ninety-third time that evening, I vetoed Lizard's suggestion that I call "my policeman" so firmly that she actually didn't nag me about it. Then I managed to squeeze in a quick shower and a slow bourbon before falling into bed just before midnight.

My last coherent thought before sleep hit was to wonder what I knew that I didn't know. That somebody else knew I knew. Or that I didn't know, but they thought I knew.

On second thought, I guess maybe it wasn't as coherent a thought as all that. Blame it on the spaniel wrapped around my head; I'm sure all that fur muffled my brain activity.

I'm sure that by now you've figured it out; chapter, verse, and murderer. And, in addition, are probably wondering how I could *not* know. Good question, especially as the whole thing seemed so obvious once the penny finally dropped. It was, after all, a pretty simple murder for a pretty simple reason—just as Lieutenant Vic Kosciusko had said it would probably be.

But remember, please, as you're chiding me for incredible denseness, that hindsight is a wonderful thing, and that distance lends not only enchantment, but clarity, to the view.

And that I—and, may I add, the police—still lacked the vital piece of information that would complete the puzzle, and let us all see what a simple pattern the design really was.

CHAPTER TEN

SATURDAY, AND SUNDAY TOO

Although I had fallen into bed in the state known as "legally dead," I didn't sleep as late into the next morning as I'd have liked. Mothers of young children and temporary custodians of young dogs don't usually have the luxury of what our British cousins call "a good lie-in." By the time I'd taken Heather and the spaniel for a walk, and fed both of them breakfast—oddly enough, when I opened the kitchen cabinet, I found a small bag of dog food next to the Cheerios box—and made time for a large cup of very strong and very sweet coffee, I felt semi-human again. Certainly human enough to speak civilly, even to Brittany Davis.

So as soon as the hour was decent (I still have this old-fashioned notion that one should not phone a residence before 9:00 a.m. or after 9:00 p.m., unless specifically invited to so do) I pulled the sacred Davis home phone number out of my wallet and dialed. After twelve rings, I hung up.

At lunchtime, I tried again. After twenty rings, I hung up. Then I took Heather and Doggie over to the park and let them exhaust each other for an hour. I called Brittany again at 3:00. This time I waited thirty rings, and set the phone down rather harder than the phone really liked; still, the plastic didn't actually crack.

"Doesn't that d—" I glanced over at the couch; found two pairs of wide brown eyes staring at me, and changed

175

words in mid-syllable, "—dratted woman have an answering machine?" I demanded of the telephone. Honestly, you'd think someone like Davis would have the latest tech-toys; he'd had the most up-to-date model of wife, after all.

Heather spent the rest of the afternoon drawing pictures of dogs of a breed apparently known as the Clairol King Charles Spaniel, to judge by their vivid and eclectic coloration. I spent the rest of the afternoon alternating reading *New York Magazine* with dialing the Davis phone number and letting the phone ring until I got bored listening to it. The spaniel spent the afternoon asleep in the sun on the windowseat.

My last call in my attempt to contact the Widow Davis on Saturday was made at 9:00 p.m.

On Sunday, my first call to the Davis Residence was made at precisely 9:01 a.m., the earliest possible moment that could be remotely considered civilized. No answer.

I spent most of Sunday helping Brenda Frostheim sort and toss papers, magazines, and a lot of old cookie boxes, mostly empty. The ones that weren't empty before Heather Melissa and the determinedly Unnamed Spaniel found them were polished cleaner than Martha Stewart's counter by the time Brenda and I hauled the dog's head out of the boxes.

"She is *such* a cutie," Brenda said. "And *so* smart, and good with the cats."

"If you mean she's smart enough to keep out of claw range while barking wildly, then yes, she's good with the cats. Brenda, honey, just how many back issues of *Soldier of Fortune* do you need, anyway?"

"What?" Brenda stared at the stack of magazines as if hoping they would suddenly turn into something more useful—like her next manuscript, typed and delivered to Margo. "Oh, all of them. But it would be nice if they were in some sort of order."

This last was said with the wistful tone usually reserved for the expression of such likely desires as winning Lotto and bumping into Harrison Ford on the street corner.

"I'll put them in chronological order," I announced, and proceeded to do so, while Heather piled cookie boxes, Spaniel sniffed around the baseboards seeking prey in the form of stray crumbs, and Brenda analyzed the Dayborne murder thus far. I'd given her chapter and verse on the anonymous letter-writer's grievance against Davis, and on the Dear Departed's widow's hissy-fit over the checkbook.

"She did it," Brenda announced, standing with an armful of lined yellow paper. "Poison is a woman's weapon." She regarded the paper in her arms longingly. "Maybe I should file this—"

"Trash," I ordered firmly. "Honey, even you can't read those notes. You already tried twice, remember?" And as they seemed to be for a book that had been published three years ago, I was pretty sure they could go to that great Shredder in the Sky.

"Who did what?" Heather asked, and Brenda and I promptly pretended we had no idea what we'd been talking about. The Dear Little Dog helped by suddenly discovering a fallen sofa cushion and loudly alerting us to the Grave Danger this posed to Civilization as Spaniel Knew It.

By the time we had the dog bribed to silence (Lorna Doones work wonders) and Heather diverted to collecting fallen magazines, murder was on our minds, all right, but we were thinking a little closer to home than Dayborne. However, Brenda was delighted to see her *Soldier of Fortune* set neatly arranged, and enchanted when I mentioned that my brother could be contacted via one of the cannily-worded classified ads run in that magazine, Heather Melissa was delighted when Brenda showed her a picture in an art book of King Charles II with a spaniel that looked Just Like Ours, and I was pleased to see Brenda's floor at long last.

At suppertime, I called the presumably bereft widow again. I also attempted to reach the Widow at 7:00, at 8:00, and at 9:00. Perhaps Brenda was right, and Brittany Davis had poisoned her husband so she could abandon her dog with a comparative stranger and run off with, I imagined, a lover who knew *The Joy Of Sex* better than he (or she; one must be broadminded and modern, after all) knew the complete text of the Securities and Exchange Commission Regulations. If that was the case, I suspected no jury of Brittany's true peers would ever convict her. At least of murder.

My last call to La Davis was made at 11:00 at night. There was still no answer.

"Don't look at me like that," I told the spaniel as I climbed into bed and shoved her off my pillow. I thought of setting my clock for 4:00 a.m. and calling Brittany *then*, but decided against it. I'd like to say that my better nature triumphed, but what actually triumphed was exhaustion.

It had been a long hard week.

CHAPTER ELEVEN

MONDAY MORNING AGAIN

Monday morning was not fun. I woke up late and with a raging headache. Heather fussed over her breakfast as if it were the Treaty of Versailles and Waldo ran my last pair of pantyhose. Determined to hand the spaniel (whom Lizard was now calling Moll Flanders and whom Heather was now calling Lady Tramp) back to her actual owner, I decided to take the dog to Dayborne with me in the hopes of persuading Brittany Davis to come and get her. And if I couldn't do that, I swore I was going to leave the spaniel with Dayborne Security and let *them* deal with the problem.

That decision meant that instead of taking a subway that stalled once between 42nd and 34th, and again between 34th and 23rd, I took a cab (a necessary expense I probably couldn't bill to Dayborne) that became hopelessly trapped in traffic just past 14th Street. I got to my desk at 9:05, and Fran regarded me reprovingly.

"You're late," she said, as if I didn't already know that. She didn't even bother to ask why I brought the dog.

"I was here damn late Friday night," I snapped. "It works out. Is Ms. Eaton in her office?"

"She's taken a personal day." Fran's tone of long-suffering reproof suggested that Carolyn Eaton flung Dayborne's hours heedlessly to the winds of time. Certainly you'd never guess, upon hearing Fran's statement, that Carolyn Eaton, like most Dayborne vice presidents, regularly clocked in fifty- or sixty-hour weeks.

But since Carolyn Eaton wasn't going to be at Dayborne today, I couldn't blow off some steam by ever-so-sweetly letting Ms. AVP know how late I'd waited up for her nonexistent work on Friday night.

I complained, instead, to Fran, who said, "That's what we're paid for," in chiding tones suitable for use in a kindergarten.

She added that business always took precedence over personal affairs, which I thought was such an idiotic position that I stopped talking to her, swearing mentally that if Fran said one had to be prepared to Go The Extra Mile, I'd get up and feed her the Dictaphone tape she was working on. I wondered who'd given her the tape, but not very hard. I supposed that with Davis gone, Fran's flying fingers were fair game for anyone in the department who needed some typing done. That was Our Girl Fran the Team Player: conscientious to the end.

I tied the spaniel's leash to one of the legs of my desk and had just picked up the phone to call Brittany Davis when Nelson Branagh rang me, asking me to come to his office immediately. For a moment, I wondered if the flyers I'd rashly strewn over the twenty-first floor bulletin boards were about to be laid before me while I was castigated for reckless endangerment of corporate culture. But the Branagh emergency turned out to be a burning desire to learn whether I'd made a decision about Joining The Dayborne Family.

Using every bit of self-control at my command, I said neither "I'd rather join the Addams Family, thanks," nor "I'd rather join the French Foreign Legion Camp Followers Corps." Instead, I murmured, Thank You, But No; You See, I Had A Child and . . .

Branagh didn't quite blanch, but I could see his sudden desperate wish to recall his offer to me. Affirmative action regulations notwithstanding, corporations distrust anyone who has an interest in life other than the corporation's bottom line, and are leery of hiring same. Women with young children almost always fall into this category, so when I began apologetically explaining how I couldn't possibly give Dayborne the dedication it truly deserved from its employees, Nelson Branagh was truly, deeply understanding as I ladled sugar so thickly on my excuses I nearly gave myself instant diabetes. Mother would have been proud of me.

On my way back to my desk, I detoured past a couple of the bulletin boards. Not a bright pink flyer to be seen. Dayborne Efficiency Strikes Back.

After *that,* I'd barely settled myself back at my desk and picked up the phone again when Brittany Davis saved me the trouble of dialing. She came stalking in on heels high enough to give the average woman a nosebleed, once more demanding Davis's checkbook.

"Because it's not at the house and the police don't have it, so you hand it over right now, you—" Descriptive nouns failed our Brittany at this point; she simply waved her hands at Fran like a demented semaphorist.

"I'm sorry, Mrs. Davis. I don't have it."

Fran didn't sound particularly sorry, actually. She continued typing away, ignoring Brittany. Well, the golden thread that had connected them (Davis) had snapped; Fran's loathing of the second Mrs. Davis need no longer be hidden.

"Then where the hell is it?" Brittany demanded of the world at large.

"I don't know," Fran said, and logged out of her document. She picked up a manila folder and walked away from her desk, leaving Brittany standing there with her beautifully-glossed mouth half-open.

"Well," said Brittany. *"Well."* She swung her gaze at me; I shook my head.

"I'm just a temp here," I reminded her. The hell with a sense of duty, I thought; I was calling Holly at MOP and telling her to get me out of this madhouse. Maybe Holly could get me a nice quiet stint in a boiler factory instead.

But before I did that, there was the vexed question of my involuntary dog-sitting. I bent and unwound the rhinestone-studded leash from the desk leg and stood up. "By the way, you know I've still got your sweet little dog," I began, and Brittany cut me off almost in mid-word.

"Great, fine. I'm glad you like her. Now, about my husband's checkbook—"

My turn to interrupt; it's hard to stifle a Southern girl. "Of course I like her, she's a dear little thing, and I'm sure you miss her dreadfully. Here you are." I started to walk towards Brittany to hand her the gaudy leash, only to be halted as the length of rhinestone-embellished velveteen stretched taut. I glanced down; the same spaniel who flung herself upon total strangers as if they were long-lost lovers had planted her furry rear end on the carpet in an admirable impersonation of a hydrastone puppy. She looked up at me and the tip of her tail wagged slightly.

For a moment, Brittany stared at me as if I were speaking pure Klingon or some other outlandish and incomprehensible tongue. Then she shrugged. "If you don't want it, take it to the pound." She didn't look at the dog at all.

"You're upset; you don't mean that," I suggested. "She's so sweet and quiet—"

"That damn dog is the biggest pain in the ass—doesn't do a thing I tell it and always licking, licking—and honestly, the shedding! All over my clothes—it was Abe's idea, and do you think he ever lifted one finger to help with it?" From Brittany's embittered tone, you'd think her late husband had saddled her with a dozen Great Danes, rather than one handbag-sized spaniel. (Okay, one spaniel the size of a *large* handbag, but still . . .) "No. Of course not. And I don't give a damn if the President's got one. Is the President going to walk it?"

"You don't want her," I said, to make sure I had this perfectly clear.

"I hope it chokes," Brittany said. "You want it, you keep it. Look, I'll send you its papers—it's got papers, you know," she added, as if this were some inducement.

At this point, I didn't care if the spaniel had magazines; I wasn't handing her back to Brittany Davis, who would dump the sweet little thing off at the nearest dog pound. (Which in New York City is the SPCA up at East 92nd Street.) "Fine," I said, recklessly committing myself to yet another unexpected and potentially disastrous relationship. I slipped the loop at the end of the leash over my wrist and then scribbled my address on a piece of notepaper and handed it to Brittany. "Send them here. By the way, what's her name?"

"Precious," said Brittany, which revolted me on so many levels I was nearly speechless. "Not that it pays any attention. It's the stupidest damn dog—"

"Not like Lassie?" I offered, and Brittany seemed relieved that I understood. She reverted to her obsession, the Master's Checkbook. She still wanted it and didn't intend to leave without it in her possession.

"But really, I don't know where it is," I kept assuring

her, and tried at last to cut the circular conversation short by making a sensible suggestion about the checkbook. "Look, Brittany, if the checkbook's really lost, why not talk to your bank? I bet they can—"

"*You* look." Brittany leaned both hands flat on my desk and glared at me with the demented look of a frustrated ferret. "I want that checkbook. I know damn well it's not lost. I know *she's* got it. I'm tired of getting checks filled out by *her*—I bet she even forged his signature on them. Anything to save Abe a lick of work. It's *my* checkbook now. It's my money. So tell her to hand it over."

I hate being towered over, especially by whippet-like girl-women in too-trendy designer clothes. "Brittany, I don't know what you're talking about," I said patiently. I weighed my next words carefully for, oh, let's say a tenth of a second, because frankly, at that point I didn't care if I ever saw my spaniel's "papers." "And guess what, honey? *I don't care.*"

The phone rang; I answered it. Guess who? The police, wanting to know if I could come down to Police Plaza again. They'd picked up a man who fit the description I'd given them of yesterday's visitor. Would I please—?

I would, and I did, and it was.

The only good thing about the experience was running into Vic, who'd come down to have a look at his new suspect. After the day I'd already had, I was glad to see a nice large friendly policeman. Vic was a particularly large one, and he certainly seemed friendly.

"Hello, Mrs. Upshaw," he said, smiling. Then, regarding me closely, he asked, "Is this what they call a Bad Hair Day?" He glanced down at the spaniel I was holding. Fortunately, the Spaniel Formerly Known As Precious was a compact little thing, and also possessed a sweet curiosity and apparently enjoyed new experiences. And equally fortunately, Lieutenant Victor Kosciusko knew when *not* to ask a question.

"Very," I told him. "Yes, that's him all right. Cassius."

"A lean and hungry look," Vic agreed.

"Is that all you're going to say about him?" I asked, rather crossly.

Since I'd discovered this suspect all by myself—well, to be perfectly accurate, he'd found me, but the principle remained the same—I thought I deserved a little information. I explained this at great length to Lieutenant Kosciusko.

"All right," he said at last, when I slowed for breath. Laughter rippled just beneath the words. "His name's Desmond Philipps; he's admitted to sending anonymous letters. He's not admitting to murder, though."

"Why was he sending Davis anonymous letters?"

"Davis got Philipps fired from Highlines Enterprises. That was a few of Davis's jobs back—by the way, did you know Davis's corporate nickname was The Terminator?"

I shook my head. "All right, I'll bite. Why?"

"Apparently he was frequently brought in to help with what they call downsizing."

"In English, that means, 'You're fired'," I put in.

"Right. Anyway, Davis was apparently a genius at booting executives out the door, contract or no contract—and making sure the downsizing company didn't have to pay too much for the privilege of booting."

"So their golden parachutes—"

"Didn't open. Or at least, not enough to cushion the fall."

A golden parachute is the flip side of the golden handcuffs. The handcuffs are inducements—bribes, if you like—to stay. The parachute is the negotiated severance package a high-powered executive gets when he leaves his firm. If too many executives jump ship at once, there can be a major drain on company resources.

"So Davis downsized Philipps, and Philipps wrote him hate mail."

"Just to relieve his feelings, Philipps says. It might even be true. Philipps is pretty bitter about the whole thing. Apparently he can't get another job paying anything like what he used to be making."

That's because everyone's "downsizing" to "streamline their operation." Then everyone wonders why no one can find a job.

"Do you think Philipps killed Davis?" I asked.

"He's on our little list, of course. I admit it's hard to see how he could have managed to poison the coffee, though it's possible he could have, I suppose. Barely," Vic added, after a moment's thought.

"Who's at the top of the list?"

"Now, Mrs. Upshaw, you know I can't tell you that." He smiled. "What about you? Any brilliant deductions?"

"No—and at this point," I said darkly, "I'd happily murder the entire staff of Dayborne myself."

"I'll bear that in mind if they all suddenly drop dead," Vic declared with admirable gravity.

"You do think you'll get the murderer, don't you?" And then Vic would call me. And I would say—

"Oh, yes. I think so." He hesitated, ever so slightly, then went on, "You see, either murders are fairly easy to solve—and it's just a question of getting proof for the jury—or they're impossible. When they're easy—oh, somebody tries to explain too much instead of keeping his mouth shut, or tries too hard to cover his tracks when it's not necessary. Or when they get greedy and try for an even bigger score. It's usually little things that trip murderers up."

"And when they're not easy?"

"Then we have to hope that someday someone walks in and confesses. Or gets picked up for another crime six states away and we get a match. Sheer luck."

"That's not very reassuring," I said.

"No. It isn't. We do our best."

I said I guessed he did, and mentioned (casually) that it was almost lunchtime. I probably even looked up at him slantwise through my mascara-darkened lashes. (Even us failed Southern belles flirt. It's a gift—rather like something bestowed by the Fairy Maleficent at our christenings.)

Vic looked down at me, thanked me for my civic-minded concern and cooperation, and reminded me (gravely) that the Davis investigation wasn't over yet.

"I know," I said, and set down the spaniel; we both walked over to the viewing room door. I opened the door and paused, my hand on the doorknob and my body half-turned back towards him. My turn to be Inspector Columbo; I smiled. "Oh, and by the way, Lieutenant Kosciusko, you might try asking Desmond Philipps where he was last night about nine-thirty."

"He was here in custody," Vic said. "Why?"

Like anyone else, I hate acting as Straight Man; I'm afraid I closed the door rather harder than strictly necessary on my way out.

And then it *was* lunchtime, and a busy day had already been had by all. It was just about to get lots busier, too, but fortunately I didn't know that in advance.

Chapter Twelve

Monday Afternoon

I suppose I should have taken the dog back up home, but I knew Lizard was out until late evening, and I also didn't want to spend the money on yet another cab. So I spent an unrushed lunch hour walking my new dog in Battery Park and sharing a hot dog lunch with her, and we both returned to Dayborne, where I found only a small pile of only semi-urgent work awaiting me. Apparently while I'd been out the Dayborne Corp. Res. & Accts. elves had been only moderately busy; even at Dayborne, the pace slowed slightly in the summer.

So the afternoon began quietly; I typed and the spaniel slept under my desk. Later I decided the day had just been lulling me, letting me catch my breath before flinging more slings and arrows in my direction. Perhaps this is too anthropomorphic of me, as well as pretty damn solipsistic. Still . . .

I edited a couple of documents and printed them out. I typed up a memo from a Dictaphone tape. I filed.

If you wonder where all this work came from, with the boss dead, remember, please, that Davis had headed a department staffed by a dozen people, none of whom was shy about petitioning Fran Jenkins, the dear-departed department head's executive secretary, for the use of my time now that death had so conveniently made that time available. Some of them, after all, actually had to *share* a secretary—

an indication of low caste that made the poor dears cross. This did make me consider the theory that one of the lesser barracuda—one of the overworked and secretary-poor junior vice presidents—had murdered Davis to get access to secretarial services. Unfortunately, I was forced to reject this attractive theory; the average jury would never buy that as motivation.

As I said, relative quiet reigned for about two hours. The moderate but steady flow of clerical work at least meant I didn't have to talk to Fran. I could not, frankly, imagine that the two of us had anything further to talk about.

As soon as I had a chance, I called my placement counselor at MOP. Holly wasn't exactly bowled over with astonishment to hear that I wanted out of Dayborne, and promised me a new assignment for tomorrow.

"If you want one, that is. Maybe you need a few days off?"

"Depends on what you can get me, Holly. I admit starting next Monday would be nice. And something quiet and low key this time, please? I'm feeling fragile."

"Okay," Holly agreed.

I could practically see her brown curls bouncing. I knew she'd be nodding vigorously, taking notes, and flipping through her files to see who needed what, and how I'd fit into MOP's current matchmaking game. Matching the temp to the job is an art, not a science.

"Oh, and by the way," I said, just before I hung up, "I want to go over the Dayborne billing and make sure it's correct. This past week's been a bit weird, hours-wise."

"No problem," Holly caroled; nothing ever seemed to be a problem for Holly. "Anything else?"

"Yes. They tried to hire me permanent."

"Oh, did they?" Holly's voice indicated that Dayborne Was Going To Be Sorry. It's very bad form to try to hire

189

temps out from under their agency. There are proper ways to acquire a temporary employee as an addition to your corporate family, and improper ones. The proper ones involve the company that wants the temp paying a hefty fee to her agency to acquire her permanently. The improper ones involve such hair-splitting as waiting until the temp's gone to temp at some other company for a week or so, then hiring her.

Which is not, technically, the same thing as hiring her while she's temporarily employed by your company.

Temp agencies hate this technicality. It's hard enough for them to keep good personnel as it is.

"I just thought you'd like to know," I told Holly. "I'm sure they'd have talked to you about it if I'd been interested in their offer."

"Of *course* they would have," Holly cooed in my ear. Probably they would have, too; Dayborne does everything by the book. As long as you're reading the same book they are, you and Dayborne will get along just fine.

Don't get me wrong—Dayborne's a fine example of its kind. And for some people, it's a great place to be.

I wasn't one of them. Dayborne Ventures, Inc. should live and be well, but I thought it was time I checked another volume out of the library of possibilities.

"Don't worry, Cornelia," Holly finished up, "I'll check around and call you back as soon as I come up with something."

"No rush. You can call me at home if you want." Just as I opened my mouth to say good-bye, my back brain made a last-minute decision which I found out about when I found myself adding, "Holly? You might as well call Dayborne personnel and tell them I'm not coming back tomorrow. Is that a problem?"

"Not for us," Holly said. "Sure, doll, I'll take care of everything—you go home and get some rest for the rest of the week. I bet you need it."

I agreed that probably I did, and we said good-bye. As I hung up the phone an invisible weight lifted from my body. There was no doubt about it, Dayborne had me thoroughly spooked by now, and the intensity of my relief at getting out of there revealed the depth of my unease. Much, much better to pack up and get the hell out of the place. Metropolitan Office Professionals would happily provide Dayborne with another temp for Monday, assuming Dayborne happened to want one. A soft thump-thump-thump by my feet made me look down to see the spaniel wagging her tail in apparent agreement.

"So you're leaving." This time Fran hadn't made any pretense of not listening, which was a minor breach of unwritten office etiquette. Since our desks faced each other across the traffic path, there was no such thing as a private phone call; in such a case, politeness dictates you pretend you haven't heard whatever the other person was saying.

Lots of times that's just plain impossible, of course. It's truly amazing what people will discuss in loud tones in the middle of an office—and then they wonder why everyone knows their personal business.

"Yes," I said. "I'm sorry, but . . ." Endeavoring to be tactful, I trailed off the sentence; Fran could finish my non-explanation any way she liked.

"Well," said Fran, "I can't say I blame you. There's no real loyalty left anywhere, anymore."

This seemed pretty harsh, considering I was only a temp to start with, but I didn't argue. I just said that, no, I guessed there wasn't.

Which pretty well settled that.

By now it was past 4:00, and I began packing up my things, preparatory to leaving forever at 5:00 sharp. Fran watched me for a few minutes, then got her handbag out of her desk and walked off down the hall. Frankly, I didn't pay her much attention, because I was too intent on making sure I wouldn't leave any of my own belongings behind.

A temp flits from job to job with never a desk to call her own. She's always subletting someone else's. It's unavoidably impersonal; the Man Without A Country has nothing on the Secretary Without A Desk. So I take some of my own things with me, to make whatever place I'm at temporarily mine. Nothing much, and nothing irreplaceable: a celadon-green ceramic vase I picked up in Chinatown which holds either pens or a flower equally well (although not simultaneously); a paperback dictionary (just in case I suddenly forget how to spell); a picture of Heather in a pewter frame (to remind me what I'm fighting for). Little things like that.

I'd gotten most of it stuffed into my tote bag when I realized I didn't have my coffee mug. This item is more frequently used to hold tea, or ice water, or even soda pop, but somehow it remains firmly and forever a coffee mug.

The mug was hardly an irreplaceable item (no, it did not have my name on it—*you* find a ready-made mug with CORNELIA on it), since I'd bought it in Lamston's a few weeks ago when I broke my last Office Coffee Mug. It was just a nice extra-large-size mug with a picture of the Brooklyn Bridge on it.

And it was *my* nice extra-large mug. I started hunting around for it because things do migrate, even in the best of offices, and came pretty quickly to the conclusion that my mug wasn't in or on the desk formerly known as mine.

So I went over to take a quick look around on Fran's.

Since I didn't really (to the best of my conscious knowledge) think she had my missing mug, I don't to this day quite understand what I was really looking for. But I thought I was looking for my coffee mug. Frankly, I didn't even quite remember when last I'd seen it; if asked, I would have sworn the mug had been on my desk all day. The spaniel trailed after me, and when she saw me peering on and under the desk, set her nose down and began sniffing industriously.

"Thanks," I said, and her tail waved even more vigorously.

My mug wasn't on Fran's desk. Or under it—I stooped to check, pushing the spaniel aside so I could get a good look. As I stood up, the little dog was up on her hind legs, her front paws resting on the handle of Fran's top right-hand desk drawer. She put her nose to the drawer and drew in breath in a long ecstatic sigh. I bet she smelled chocolate bars; smiling, I caught her collar and pulled her away—

—and her long-furred silky white paws caught in the drawer's handle. And the drawer pulled out just enough to show the desk wasn't locked.

Just enough to reveal, as I leaned over to shut the drawer again, the leather cover of the oversized desk checkbook lying inside.

Remember I said always lock your desk when you walk away from it, even if you're just going ten feet down the hall?

Of course I pulled the drawer farther open. The leather was oxblood red-brown, and gleamed as if the leather were handled often. It was Davis's checkbook, which had lived on his office credenza and which I'd seen Fran writing in half-a-dozen times. Just in case I might still be in any doubt, the name "J. Abercrombie Davis" was imprinted in the lower corner of the cover in flowing gold script.

There wasn't, of course, any reason Fran shouldn't have the checkbook. Because among many other tasks, official and personal, that she had done for her boss, she had kept Davis's personal checkbook for him.

But she told Brittany she didn't have it, my mind whispered.

Well, so what? Considering Brittany's attitude, I might not have told her right away either. *Ah,* my mind went on remorselessly, *but what did Fran tell the police? Does Vic know she has it?*

I looked down into the spaniel's soft dark eyes. "Clever girl," I said, and reached in and flipped open the checkbook. As I said, the checkbook was the big office kind, three checks to a page and a memo stub beside each check for notes. And just in case you forgot to make the notes, when you wrote a check, you automatically wrote yourself a copy on the carbonless backing slip behind the check itself.

Davis's checkbook had been beautifully tended. Each check was written out in a clear forthright hand—Fran's. They were signed with the angry scrawl that Davis passed off as a signature.

The balance was consistently high: very high. The entries looked pretty standard: payments to American Express, Visa, Diners Club, Carte Blanche. Telephone, electric, car. And every two weeks, a check for two thousand dollars written out to Brittany Davis. The notation beside those said, in Fran's primmest script, "Mrs. Davis's personal allowance."

I suddenly felt a great deal more sympathy for Brittany Davis than I'd been willing to grant her before. Getting an allowance doled out to her as if she were a child, not an allegedly equal partner in a marriage—Although four thousand dollars a month should be enough to squeak by on, since Brittany wasn't paying for food or rent. Or maybe she was. How did I know?

I hoped Brittany had had the sense to save most of her allowance. An allowance, after all, can be stopped at the whim of the person controlling it—and you.

Realizing I was both snooping and wasting time, I turned to the last written entries. They were dated two Fridays ago, the Friday Davis had died—yes, I'd seen Fran writing checks that afternoon. She didn't like to let bills pile up, she said. No point in paying interest as well.

American Express Corporation. White Plains Mercedes. The Rye Town Hilton. A couple of names I didn't recognize—businesses, probably. Each check properly written out, and the amount dutifully subtracted from the balance of funds remaining. Hertz Rent-A-Car. Mrs. Brittany Davis.

And Frances Jenkins.

To whom a check—the last torn off—had been made out in the amount of $12,985.17. It, too, was written out in Fran's neat hand and signed with the only semi-legible scrawl that passed as Davis's signature. The notation on the memo stub merely said "for services rendered."

It seemed an odd amount, among other oddities; I looked at the balance remaining in the account after that check was drawn.

Zero.

I will never again scoff at the use of clichés. They're clichés because they're true and accurate descriptions. When I say that my blood ran cold and my skin crawled when I looked at that, I mean exactly that. I would have sworn a frozen-footed centipede was running up my spine.

And I wasn't quite sure why. Except that something was

very, very wrong with this picture—

Before I had a chance to think through the instinctive fear of whatever it was, I heard the soft pad of footfalls coming closer, sound muffled by the thick gray carpet Dayborne had spread so lavishly over its floors. Hastily, I let the checkbook fall closed and pushed the drawer shut again.

By the time Fran was back, I was standing in front of my desk, with the spaniel jumping up and pawing at my legs in excitement. I hoped I didn't look as distraught as I felt, that my attempts to catch my breath didn't show. That I looked as normal as I ever had.

Apparently I did, because Fran merely walked up to me and said, "I know it's almost five and you like to leave right on the dot, but I brought us coffee anyway. You look like you could use some before you go, and I know I could."

As she spoke, I was trying to pull myself back to total composure, with only limited success. But frazzled as I was, I still distinctly remember thinking that was odd; Fran prided herself on drinking only herbal teas. Coffee, she'd always said, was bad for you.

She was carrying two full coffee mugs: hers and mine. She put hers in the center of her desk, on the blotter. She held mine out to me. "Here."

It seemed the image of the Brooklyn Bridge wavered slightly, as if the mug were about to slip from her fingers. Automatically, I reached out and grasped the mug before it could fall, and as I lifted the mug to a safe balance, the aroma of fresh brewed coffee hit my nose. Coffee—and a hint of something else? Something sweet, smelling elusively like burnt macaroons—

Scent, they say, is the best memory trigger. Better than sight, or touch, or sound, or taste. Maybe they're right. Because the second I smelled that coffee the answer flashed into my mind, harsh and uncompromising as a searchlight. Now I remembered what I'd known all along, and forgotten I knew—what I'd known subconsciously since last Monday, when I'd glanced down into the wastebasket in the staff kitchen and seen a blue Maxwell House coffee envelope lying there.

And had heard Fran defending what hadn't needed defending; unable to bear being thought late, even in jest. *"I always get here at eight-thirty. To make Mr. Davis's coffee. Just like I did this morning."*

But there hadn't been a gold foil envelope lying in the wastebasket with the blue one. Davis's fancy coffee came in gold foil packets. So Fran hadn't made Davis coffee that morning.

"They explain too much," Vic had said.

Hadn't made Monday morning coffee, because Davis had been dead since Friday evening, and Fran knew it.

I looked down into the cup of coffee Fran had just handed me. No empty envelope; big deal. Maybe she'd thrown the thing out somewhere else, my mind argued, unwilling to believe what it knew. But where else, and why? There was no reason to hide the envelope. It hadn't been there—

And for the rest of my life, in certain moments, I will wonder if I would have stood there with Fran in blissful ignorance and drunk that coffee if I hadn't accidentally found Davis's checkbook, and looked at that check "for services rendered," and at that balance (so carefully calculated, so neatly noted down) reading "zero."

"Or they get greedy—"

Slowly, I looked from the coffee to Fran. The expression on my face must have been a dead giveaway, because without warning Fran reached out, grabbing for the mug, her soft round face rigid with sudden panic. I jumped back, clinging to the mug with both hands; this was police evidence, now. Some of the hot coffee sloshed over my fingers and I hoped, desperately, that cyanide wasn't a contact poison. I juggled the mug from hand to hand, hastily wiping my fingers on my suit jacket.

Fran didn't try anything else; she just stood there, staring at me. "So you know," she said. "I suppose you think you're very clever." She looked fake, somehow; an especially lifelike animatronic rather than a human being.

"If I'd been clever, I would have figured it out last Monday. Well, Tuesday, actually—when the police came." I hardly recognized my own voice. "But Fran—*why?*"

It was ridiculous, and I couldn't believe we were having this conversation. I was half sure I was merely suffering through a peculiarly realistic dream from which I would momentarily awake. Fran Jenkins adored J. Abercrombie Davis. Fran followed him everywhere, as Ruth did Naomi, or a good dog its master.

There was no reason on God's green earth Fran had to answer me, of course. But she did. I don't think it was the urge to confess; I'm not at all sure, even now, that Fran ever felt guilty about what she'd done. Sorry, yes; her grief over Davis's death was quite genuine.

"He was going to ICF," Fran said in a flat little voice. "And he wasn't going to take me."

"Oh, God," I heard myself saying. I sounded faint and far away; I felt rather than heard nylon split and ladder as the spaniel pawed my leg. I wanted to reassure the little dog that I was fine, but my voice didn't seem to work quite right at the moment.

"He'd met someone new. Someone young. A Katharine Gibbs graduate."

That was Fran all over, even at the finish: anyone else would have said, "A Katie Gibbs girl." Katharine Gibbs is the oldest and most prestigious secretarial school in the country; its graduates have survived and passed a two-year course as rigorous as Marine boot camp. Fran couldn't even pretend Davis would be replacing her with an inferior product.

"He said I was out of date, and that it was time I retired." Fran stared straight ahead, seeing—oh, I don't know, maybe that long span of years she'd devoted to a one-way relationship.

"The motives are usually pretty simple. Money, or passion—"

Davis had wanted to dump her, and Fran refused to be dumped the way she'd watched him dump his first wife, and all the people he'd fired so efficiently for his various employers.

So she'd killed him.

Against my will pity welled up, filling me with sorrow. *Poor Fran.* For a moment, murder almost seemed reasonable; poetic justice.

But only for a moment. Because once begun, murder doesn't stop. In my hand I held the ultimate proof.

"Or tries too hard to cover his tracks, when it's not necessary—"

Or in this case, her tracks. Because if Fran hadn't offered me that cup of coffee, because she was afraid that I'd solved the mystery, I wouldn't have remembered. And finally figured it out.

I'd almost solved the mystery with my own death. Fran had tried to kill me, and she knew Heather was only three—

"I left you coffee on Friday," Fran added, "but you didn't drink it." Faint reproach colored her voice; *I* was the uncooperative one.

"No. By the time I wanted some, it was burned stale. I poured it down the sink." Oddly, I was too furious to be afraid, but I knew I didn't dare let myself release that bone-deep anger; I had to stay calm, and hang on to the evidence in my coffee cup. I glanced down; the spaniel, her brow furrowed, sniffed the air as if testing the coffee's scent. I tried one last question, partly to test my own self-control. "Fran—were you waiting outside my apartment Friday night? To see if I—ever came home?"

But Fran didn't seem to have anything else to say, and I suppose the answer was irrelevant now. Without responding, Fran turned away and began, with her usual methodical attention to detail, to clear off her desk, closing up the office for the night.

"Fran," I said. "Fran, I've got to call the police."

She didn't pay any attention to me, just kept turning off machines and locking drawers. She didn't even remove the checkbook from her desk to take with her.

"Fran—"

"I'm going home now," Fran said, and walked calmly out past my desk and out the doors as I stared after her, still unable to really believe it. Fran, of all people. A part of my mind tried to tell me I was wrong; mistaken.

But I wasn't. Fran Jenkins had committed murder. Murder premeditated, and pretty cold-blooded.

I remembered holding Harriet Benson rigid in my arms, watching her skin fade to blue as she fought for breath after using the coffee pot that Fran had hastily switched for Davis's. And I remembered that half-full coffee pot sitting there on the hot plate in the staff lounge Friday night. Just sitting there, waiting. Waiting for anyone who happened along, like another late worker or one of the cleaning crew, and fancied a quick cup of coffee to wake them up—

A careless way to kill. Sloppy. And undiscriminating. There was no real guarantee I'd be the first—let alone the only—one to drink that particular brew. And if I'd walked in and found a dead body lying beside the coffeemaker, I very probably would not, then, have drunk a cup myself. It seemed unlikely.

Very carefully, I set the cup of coffee Fran had given me down in the center of my desk. With equal care, I pulled a felt-tip marker out of my desk drawer and printed on a sheet of paper, in big block letters, DO NOT TOUCH. I placed the paper over the top of the mug, folded it down over the sides, and slid a rubber band around both to keep the paper in place. Just to make sure, I then set the mug very carefully in the large bottom desk drawer where I usually kept my purse. I slid the drawer very slowly closed and locked the desk.

Then, walking very carefully and trailed by a solicitous spaniel I didn't dare touch, I went to the ladies' room and washed my hands over and over with soap and hot water until they hurt.

After that, I called the police. To my amazement, neither my hand nor my voice shook.

Too much.

Once again, the police were admirably prompt. At least, I guess they were. Anyway, the next thing that made much of an impression on me was Detective Morton standing in front of my desk and Vic kneeling beside me while the spaniel sat on my lap with her paws on my shoulders and licked my face.

"Cornelia," Vic was saying, "are you all right?" He was saying it patiently, as if he'd been repeating the same words for a while.

"Oh," I said. "Here you are. Fran killed Davis and she just tried to poison me. I saved the coffee for you to analyze. It's in the drawer," I told Vic. I also assured him that I was fine, just fine. And then I maturely and soberly proceeded to have hysterics. I distinctly remember sobbing against Vic's chest, which was broad and solid and eminently suited to such activity. All my Southern belle ancestors would have been real proud of me.

Chapter Thirteen

Tuesday Afternoon

In a fictional murder mystery of the proper sort, Fran would have gone home and drunk a cyanide cocktail herself, thereby paying for her crime and providing a tidy ending to her bleak little tragedy. Also thereby saving the People and the State of New York a whole lot of time and money.

This being real life, Fran called a lawyer instead. By Tuesday, Fran had already been arrested and booked. She would probably be out on bail within twenty-four hours, if her lawyer had anything to say about it. Her lawyer, I'd been given to understand by Vic, had quite a lot to say about everything.

I called Holly Steinberg and told her I didn't want any more jobs *anywhere* until further notice. Eventually I'd gotten around to mentioning why, and Holly'd been livid—and also assured me, grimly, that I'd certainly get paid for the rest of the time I'd been *supposed* to be at Dayborne. I thanked her, glad I wasn't the Dayborne executive who'd be trying—vainly, if I knew Holly—to explain that Dayborne wasn't liable for murder attempts on the premises.

Holly also demanded I stay home and rest. I promised I would.

Right now I was resting on the couch in my living room, watching Heather coloring over by the window. Waldo was crouching on the windowseat growling at the pigeons on the outer sill. The pigeons weren't impressed, and kept up their steady circling, chatting to each other in an endless cooing mumble. More or less beside Waldo—just out of claw distance—sat Fancy, her nose pressed against the window-screen. Pigeons, the attitude of both Siamese and spaniel indicated, required constant surveillance. Eternal vigilance is the price of pigeons.

Yes, we at last had a name for the spaniel, for Brittany Davis, delighted to have the murder pinned on her late husband's too-devoted secretary, had remembered to messenger me the promised "papers." These turned out to be not only vet records, but registration papers. These very impressive registration and pedigree papers from something called the Cavalier King Charles Spaniel Club, USA, Inc. informed us that our unexpectedly permanent dog was officially known as Talitho King's Fancy. Her color, by the way, was described as "Blenheim."

So all other names were neatly vetoed in favor of calling her Fancy. (I'd told Lizard that Brittany Davis had been calling the dog "Precious." Lizard had made gagging noises, just as she had when, as a child, she had been confronted with something truly odious, such as creamed lima beans.) Fancy already had a new collar and leash—without rhinestones.

Anyway, I regarded this peaceful family scene placidly; I had my feet on the coffee table and a can of soda pop in my hand. Inside the can was a nice mix of Classic Coke and Rebel Yell bourbon. More of the nice mix was inside me, where it was doing its best to make itself comfortable.

Lieutenant Victor Kosciusko had pulled the big leather chair around and sat where I could see his face. He had a can of beer in his hand; occasionally he drank from it.

Vic had come by just after I'd finally managed to boot

Liz and Julian out the door, swearing I was fine, fine, fine, and the two of them should scoot. Finally—still plainly very doubtful about the wisdom of Leaving Cornelia Alone After Her Shattering Experience—as if *not* drinking poisoned coffee could hurt you—they'd gone, promising to not be late.

I was just locking up when the bell rang, and I'd flung open the door saying, "Now look, Liz, I'm *just fine*—"

And saw Vic.

"May I come in, Mrs. Upshaw?" he asked gravely; all business. "I thought you might like an update on the case."

"I thought the case was over, Lieutenant?" I replied with equal gravity.

"Well, as a matter of fact, as far as my department's concerned, it is. Now it's up to the D.A." He lifted a brown paper bag. "I brought my own beer."

"Why?" A question that probably indicates I wasn't quite as All Right as I'd been giving out. I was also leaning against the door in a drooping blossom sort of way, come to think of it.

"Because the last time I was here, I noticed you didn't have any," said Vic, and smiled at me and came in.

Waldo glared at Vic, hissed once and then ignored him studiously. Heather and Fancy both were enchanted to see him again and both wanted to sit on his lap. Heather won the competition and Fancy sulked about his ankles until Vic asked if Heather liked to color like her Aunt Lizard, and then cunningly asked her to go draw him a policeman on a horse.

"I noticed the crayons," he said, when I raised my eyebrows at him. "And I went through this stage with John. Cheer up—in a few years she'll even clean her room rather than hang around with boring grownups."

"Oh," I said, considering this. Well, at least he wasn't put off by the thought of children, at any rate. Nor by dogs; Fancy had scrambled up and flung herself backwards across his lap so he could rub her furry white stomach, which Vic was obligingly doing. "Vic, are you ever going to tell me about the murder, or not?"

"That's why the runaround with the crayons," Vic said. "Unless you want Heather listening to every word?"

Come to think of it, I guessed I didn't. "You're—duplicitous."

Vic smiled into his beer. I considered what I'd said, but frankly, "duplicitous" sounded just fine to me, so I went on. "Did you know the murderer was—was Fran all along, or did I solve the case for you?"

I spoke lightly; flip and glib. I refused to think about the week I'd spent working just across the aisle from a poisoner.

"Yes and no," Vic said. "She was always a good bet for it. No one else had so much access to both the method and the opportunity. What was baffling us was motive. She didn't seem to have one."

"Motive, method, and opportunity," I said. "If you know how, you know who, and if you know who—"

Here I stopped, as I seemed to be getting rather tangled up and it didn't seem worth the energy to begin over.

"At that point, you've solved the case," Vic pointed out kindly. "But in the Davis murder—well, poison makes it harder. For us, of course. Easier for the murderer."

"Of course," I said, to show I was following all this technical criminology with perfect ease and assurance.

"Anyway, even though nobody had a really good alibi for the time—too wide an opportunity window to drop the poison in the pot—his secretary was in the perfect position to do it. So of course we were looking at her hard. But frankly, she seemed devoted to him."

"She was," I said. "Totally." And shivered, because too much of anything is not too good, as an old children's song tells us. In this case, too much devotion had killed a man.

"So—no motive," said Vic, and drank some beer. "Anyway, we'd already talked to the people at Davis's new firm—"

"ICF. Was that how you—"

"Made the connection? Well—yes. You helped, though."

"I did?" I said hopefully.

"You did," he assured me with every appearance of sincerity. "There are so many facts in any case—most of them totally irrelevant—that things sometimes fall through mental cracks and get half lost. And the Davis murder wasn't the only case Homicide had on its plate this week, you know."

"So?" I prompted.

"So something you said nagged at me until I finally remembered it. And then I called the head of Davis's new department at ICF—they're devastated to lose him, by the way; can't imagine who can possibly take his place—"

"They'll think of someone," I said dryly.

"Probably; not my problem, thank God. Anyway, I asked Johnson Perry—that's the ICF man—if Davis was bringing his own secretary with him, or if ICF was providing him with one. And Perry said—"

"That Davis wasn't bringing a secretary!" I finished triumphantly.

"Wrong. He was. Which seemed to be that. But then I had a brainstorm and I asked Perry to describe her. Which he did. Quite thoroughly."

"And it wasn't Fran," I said.

"It certainly wasn't. That was when I was pretty sure our

Miss Jenkins was the murderer."

"So, Mr. Holmes, when were you absolutely sure?"

"When we analyzed the mug of coffee she gave you," Vic said. "There was enough cyanide in it to kill a horse."

I guess I'd had maybe a little bit more Rebel Yell than I'd thought. Because it took me a long time of staring at Vic before I started to shake.

It didn't take Vic any time at all to haul me onto his lap. He put his arms around me. "It's all over, Cornelia. You did great. Just don't do it again, okay?"

I leaned my head against his shoulder, and pointed out that I hadn't wanted to do it this time. My foray into amateur detection was all Davis's fault.

"And the situation," I pointed out, "isn't likely to arise again."

At this point Heather trotted over and stared at us with big, round, innocent eyes, and asked why was Mommy sitting on that man's lap and what were we doing?

"Nothing, unfortunately," said Vic.

"Little pitchers," I said, and shoved myself up. I was oddly unsteady on my feet (I could *not* have had *that* much Rebel Yell); Vic braced the palm of his hand against my hip, supporting me.

"Why don't you go wash your face?" he suggested.

"And then you'll finish the wrap-up?" I demanded suspiciously.

"I promise. Go on. Heather will keep me company, won't you, Heather?"

"No!" Heather promptly exclaimed, and ran back off to her crayons. After plopping herself down, she slanted a glance to see if Vic was watching, and then began coloring with enough energy to power half Manhattan.

Vic smiled over his beer, and I took myself off to splash cold water on my face. On the way back, I hung over the refrigerator door, calculating.

"I do not," I announced with great clarity, after I'd flung myself down on the couch and picked up my soda can once more, "know *what* we're going to have for dinner."

"I do," said Vic. "I'm taking you out. And Heather too, of course."

I didn't argue; never argue with policemen. "I still don't know how she could get cyanide. I mean, surely they don't sell it anywhere?"

"You can make it, if you're determined. It's not, unfortunately, all that difficult. A number of fruit pits contain it, for example, and so do some pesticides and metal-plating solutions. And if you're going to poison someone, cyanide is certainly worth the trouble to extract it. Fast and infallible except in very, very rare cases."

"So—" I brooded over my soda can, considering the events of the past week. "So Fran poisoned Davis's coffee Friday afternoon. And then just waited—"

"Until the discovery of the body—stalling that discovery off as long as possible."

"Which was pretty long, because Davis was such a total sh—" I glanced over at my industrious little darling with the ever-listening ears and changed what I'd been going to say to, "—sugar-pie that no one dared interrupt him in his inner sanctum."

"Exactly. And she was lucky, too, because Davis certainly provided us with plenty of suspects. His wife. His ex-employees. His co-workers. Still, as I said, usually murder is simple. The obvious person in the obvious place—"

"Commits the obvious crime?" I finished brightly.

"Right. Case closed. Now it's the D.A.'s baby." Contented as a big cat, Vic stretched and took another pull at his beer.

"Vic—*was* she waiting outside my apartment Thursday night?"

"Maybe—she hasn't said. And if she was, and saw you when you were supposed to be dead at Dayborne—a pretty random chance, that—"

"Sloppy," I said concisely, which seemed to please him.

"Exactly. Anyway, even she probably didn't know what she was going to do when she saw you. Maybe nothing."

"I didn't really see anything. Actually," I said consideringly, "I panicked."

"More people should panic, then; they'd live longer. I call your reaction common sense—although I don't know why; it doesn't seem to be particularly common. You and your friends did exactly the right thing."

This was said with warm approval; I smiled. "I panicked when I saw that check, too—it was just so—so creepy. Like I'd fallen into the *Twilight Zone*."

For $12,985.17. Clearing the account precisely.

For services rendered.

"Cornelia?"

"Here," I said, and added, slowly, "I guess she thought she deserved it. The money. After what he'd done." I looked over at Vic, who plainly didn't quite understand what, precisely, Davis had done. "You see, executives get golden parachutes. Executives get payouts and stock options. Secretaries get two weeks' notice. Unless their company's real, real generous. Dayborne was going to give her a month's salary."

For a moment we both drank in silence; I heard the damn pigeons cooing and Waldo's continuous low threats. Heather's crayons whispered vigorously over her drawing paper. Trying to regain Vic's attention, Fancy waved her paws and licked the air enthusiastically.

"Vic, will Fran get to keep that money?" I finally asked.

"That last check she wrote? Well, it might be possible to get her for grand larceny and forgery. On the other hand," said Vic in a fair-minded fashion, "you'd have to prove the check was written after Davis's death or without his knowledge."

"She wrote all his checks," I said. I thought of Fran sitting there that Friday afternoon, neatly and dutifully writing out Davis's checks, whether Davis was dead or not—

"And signed them, too, apparently."

I nodded. I'd known that; most good secretaries can create a reasonable facsimile of their boss's signature. Fran's forgery work was better than that; you couldn't tell her version of Davis's scrawl from his.

Scribbling Carolyn Eaton's initials onto the memo that had kept me there on Friday night must have been a piece of sugar cake. Of course, I'd been gullible. Too willing, perhaps, to believe the worst of bosses in general. And to believe the best of secretaries. Fran had murdered Davis because of passion; because she loved him and he was abandoning her.

But she'd been willing to kill me for her own convenience. To tidy up an end that was loose only in her own mind.

"Cornelia," Vic said again, very gently.

"I'm okay. So what happens now?"

"Now the press will probably have a field day. This thing's got Movie of the Week written all over it." Vic sounded disgusted. "And Ms. Jenkins will probably get off on some fancy plea of temporary insanity or irresistible impulse. She's gotten herself a damn good lawyer."

For a moment Vic looked almost crossly at his beer; then he shrugged. "Again, not my problem. Thank God."

A damn good lawyer cost damn good money; I wondered just how much Frances Jenkins had socked away. Twelve-thousand-something-dollars would barely pay for a damn good lawyer's opening statement to a jury.

He drank his beer and I drank my soda-pop-and-bourbon and thought about what he'd said.

Temporary insanity? I didn't think so. I thought Frances Jenkins had killed J. Abercrombie Davis because, however briefly, she had become temporarily sane.

And had seen, not what he'd done to her, but what she'd let him do. Just as I'd once let Ravenal—

I shivered again, and Vic leaned forward, setting his beer can down beside the Service's outrageously malformed teapot. "Look," he said, "what about dinner?"

I was cold all over; doubt is a chilling emotion. "I don't think—" I began. Then I stopped myself.

Not what Ravenal'd done, but what I'd let him do. I thought I'd fought free of him, but I'd been wrong. I'd been fooling myself. There hadn't been a day since his death that memory of Ravenal hadn't ruled my actions.

A few nights ago I'd thrown his ring away. That had been easy; I should have done it years ago. Now I had to make a less dramatic, harder choice.

"I don't think I feel much like going out," I said. It was true; at the moment I wasn't, quite, certain that I could stand up. (I'm *quite* sure I hadn't drunk that much bourbon.)

"Oh." Vic sat back again, and then slid his hands around Fancy and set her gently upon the floor by his feet. "Well, I understand. I suppose—"

He had great control over his voice; it was level, non-committal. But I knew what he thought. Case over; emotions over. Cop dismissed.

It would be so easy. Just keep my mouth shut, and he'd leave. I'd be safe. . . .

And Ravenal would still be telling me what to do. It isn't true that the dead are quiet. I made my choice, and even now, that choice wasn't easy.

"So maybe you'd be ever so kind, Lieutenant, and bring something in?" My heart was pounding and I felt oddly short of breath, but I'd done it. I had. I took a long swallow out of my soda can. The mixture was pretty warm and pretty flat by now.

"Sure," said Vic. He was smiling, now, and his voice wasn't noncommittal at all. "Not a problem, Mrs. Upshaw." After the briefest hesitation he reached over to touch my left hand, his fingers resting lightly on the pale band my wedding ring had left upon my finger.

"Not a problem," I said, echoing him. And smiled.

ABOUT THE AUTHOR

Long ago, India Edghill lived in New York City and worked as a temporary secretary. Although she never found a corpse during her years as a temp, she did learn many useful things. She passed this arcane knowledge on to Cornelia Upshaw when Ms. Upshaw needed a job. Now India is a writer of fantasy short stories and historical novels. Her first historical novel, *Queenmaker*, tells the story of King David through the eyes of his queen; her second, *Wisdom's Daughter* (St. Martin's Press), retells the story of King Solomon and the Queen of Sheba. She lives in the beautiful, pollen-filled MidHudson Valley with her sister, five spaniels, six cats, and far too many books about far too many subjects.